THE WARRIOR AND HER DIVINE

GABRIELLA DENNANY

ALSO BY

Also by Gabriella Dennany

The Chronicles of Milo Bohr:

The Halls of Valhalla (book 1)

A Tale from The Halls of Valhalla:

The Warrior and Her Divine

CONTENTS

For all the fans of Thor & Loki, who feel like pop culture just hasn't given us enough of them.

This one is for you.

ONE

The bowstring twitched in Astrid's grasp.

Long ago, before she became a soldier in the Royal Guard of Asgard, Astrid watched her father whittle a bow beside a smoldering fire. He dragged the edge of the flat blade across the wood, his crooked nose following the path he traced. The wood was an ashy white, as if the sun's gaze had burnt and killed it. They were shards from the *Asketre,* silvery trees native to the woods outside Asgard's golden kingdom, where Odin's, the All-Father, rule grew clouded.

While he carved, Astrid knelt beside him, caught in a trance. It wasn't often that he was home, since he provided for the farm as a traveling merchant. When he found himself resting at their homestead, Astrid clung to him as if it were the last time. In those days, her younger sister Frey was still pressed to their mother's bosom, no older than five. Astrid, as the eldest and reaching eleven years of age, was endowed with the burden of stepping into her father's shoes one day.

"Do you know why, *mitt hjerte*[1], we use the *Asketre* to carve our bows?" he asked on one warm evening.

Astrid shook her head. "*Asketre* is cursed," she said.

"Because," he murmured, leaning closer to her ear, "while everyone else cowers at the cursed wood, we overcome our fear." He pulled away and pointed at her with the carving blade. "Tell it back to me."

"To overcome our fear."

He shook his head and grabbed her slender arms fervently. "Again."

"To overcome—"

Snap!

Her father hit the side of her face with the *Asketre*—once, sharply, and then again, heavy and intentional. "Again," he hissed, the fire illuminating his eyes.

Astrid swallowed her tears as the stinging pain erupted. She flinched as she spoke, already anticipating the next blow. "To—"

Snap!

"Again!" he shouted. "Do not wince. Do not turn away from it. Take it, straight on!" Like a madman, he bashed the bow against her face another time, pulling the wood back to see it stained red. "*Again!*"

Astrid gritted her teeth, ignoring the throbbing pulse on her temple. "To overcome our fear!"

---

1. Translation: My heart.

He lowered the *Asketre,* which was now whittled into a fine recurve bow. He rested the newly fashioned weapon against her lap with a surprisingly gentle touch. "You remember that, *mitt hjerte,* and perhaps you will survive what fate has in store for you."

As far as Astrid was concerned, fate could go suck on a goat's cock.

The memory lived on in her head thirteen years later, when all that remained of her father were decaying bones and a scar from where the *Asketre* once pummeled her. Astrid breathed in as her grip grew tense around the bow's leather-bound handle. The world ahead of her was misty, from both the tundra environment and the haunting memory clinging to the corner of her vision. Her fingers curled against the tight string and fidgeted again. The bow wobbled, the arrowhead no longer facing its target.

"Shit," she hissed.

Beside her, someone stirred.

"What is it?"

"Get back down, Ullr."

Raising himself from the icy patch upon the cliffside that they lay upon, Ullr tried to steal a glance at the gorge below. Tall Jotunn gathered in the center of their village. Surrounded by a world of sterling white ice, the giants stood out like a sore thumb, their skin as blue as the deepest parts of the sea. The male giants housed staggering antlers, making them an extra foot or two taller than the rest. They were three times the size of an average Asgardian. Astrid glanced over at Ullr.

My company is anything but the average Asgardian.

In the bright silver world of Jotunnheim, four gods of the Aesir pantheon lied in the cover of ice and snow. They were brought together beneath the god of Thunder, whose father sat upon the Bleeding Throne of Asgard as the king. Ullr, who was the lesser out of the rest of them, was simply the archer god, left to watch over Astrid during her most pivotal moment. The three others within her company were scattered around Jotunnheim, waiting for the signal to go forth with their roles in the mission.

Out of them all, Astrid was the single mortal, wrapped up in the world of gods. She often remembered the day she was brought before the Bleeding Throne, the One-Eyed All-Father watching her with an intensity that set a fire to her skin. The moment the words were uttered – "you will join my son's traveling company" – Astrid's life changed into something no mortal ever deserved.

"Odin's breath," Ullr whispered. "Are you seeing this?"

"I'm busy," she grumbled, shifting her weight as she tried to refocus on the targets. The bow trembled.

Astrid only heard rummaging before Ullr's gloved hand grasped her shoulder. He shook her fervently. She jerked her shoulder, smacking his hand away.

"You'll make me lose my concentration," she whispered.

Ullr grumbled before grabbing a hold of her again. "Get over here."

She sighed like a child. The Jotunn were moving too much, anyway. Astrid set her eyes on the chieftain, his station undeniable with the obsidian headdress he wore. The other giants gathered around him, landing claps on his shoulders and speaking rapidly.

Even at their distance, Astrid heard the quiet rumbles of their harsh and jagged language. They gathered in an Utførelse, a round clearing within their village used for meetings or religious offerings. The gorge was erected around the Utførelse perfectly, giving Astrid and the rest of her company a clear view.

Gathering her bow and quiver, Astrid shimmied to the right, where Ullr lay with his belly flat against the ice. Fur cloaks wrapped around his shoulders, the greys and whites blending in with their surroundings. The only visible patch of skin was along his eyes, but he had drawn dark ash along his unusually marbled skin. Even if it looked like meaningless streaks, Astrid knew it was anything but.

Rune sorcery.

Ullr took a second glance at her over his shoulder. "What're you staring at, spitfire?"

"Watch it with the pet names."

"Don't like them, *spitfire?*"

Astrid paused beside him, not even bothering to look over. "Does now really seem like the time for this, Ullr? We're supposed to be—"

"Relax, spitfire. Get to live as long as I have, and you can't help but have a bit of fun in the face of danger."

"Not all of us are gods."

Ullr eyed her and didn't speak for a moment.

The divide between Astrid and the rest of her company remained a tall wall between them. It didn't matter how long they fought or traveled together. Astrid was a speck in a sea of sand while they were the very stars in the sky. It wasn't often she mentioned it or even complained.

Astrid sighed, holding her bow tight beneath her chest. "What were you trying to show me?"

"So now you'd like to change the subject," Ullr mused with a smirk. "Wouldn't you, spitfire?"

Before she could even think about what she *really* wanted to say, a glimmer of light across the gorge caught her attention. On the other cliffside overlooking the Jotunn gathering, Astrid barely made out the silhouette of another archer. While she didn't want to call him a backup plan, she knew very well that he was, in fact, the backup plan for if she failed.

Not if, but *when*.

Astrid gripped her bow, the glimmer flickering in and out deliberately. She narrowed her eyes as she intercepted the code till it disappeared.

"Loki says we're losing our window," Astrid murmured. "They're going to bring him in any second now."

Ullr scoffed. "That's what I've been trying to tell you, spitfire." The god nodded toward the Utførelse with a sour expression. "He's already here."

"*Shit,*" she hissed for the second time that day.

Astrid's gaze fell back into the gorge. The blue-skinned Jotunn slammed their fists against iron shields, their jarring language sounding sharp and heavy from afar. The chieftain stood before an icy throne, slowly raising his arms. Within the sea of blue, a hunched figure was dragged in before the leader. Even in the deadly cold, the prisoner only wore a pair of worn trousers, bare feet dragging through the permanent snow.

Yanking up her sleeve, Astrid extended her arm toward Ullr. "Give me the sight rune."

"So demanding."

"Ullr!"

The god let out a throaty laugh before retrieving a small nub of what looked to be charcoal. Astrid eyed it. Rather than charcoal, it was an encasement of ash gathered at the foot of Yggdrasil, the legendary Tree of Life. The natural magic of everything that bound the Nine Realms together sat within Ullr's hands. His lazy and childish hands.

Ullr grasped her wrist and dragged the ash along her forearm. Whispers, unrecognizable as the wind rushed by, crept out from his lips. A tingling sensation sank beneath Astrid's skin as he drew, the lines looking familiar but unknown at the same time.

Astrid's hand clenched into a tight fist. Rune sorcery came easily to the gods. They were in tune with magic just by having golden blood coursing through their veins. Astrid, on the other hand, was nothing more than a mortal. Magic lingered longer on her, tainted her mind quicker. Once Ullr finished drawing, Astrid shook her head a few times, growing drunk and dizzy from the power that was never meant for her to hold.

"Got it, spitfire?" Ullr asked in a quiet voice. "I'm still training, you know. Bloody magic barely works sometimes."

Astrid squeezed her eyes shut, the sorcery finally beginning to creep toward her vision.

"Astrid?" He reached for her.

The moment his bare fingertips pressed against Astrid's naked arm, his marbled hand standing out against her deeply brown skin, divinity slipped into her. It was how it worked, in the oddest way. Divinity rubbed off against Astrid for a moment, leaving her skin shimmering and glowing with rays of light. In the same way, her mortality seeped into the god, turning his blood red for just a split second.

Astrid jerked away, his divinity calming the rushing magic that threatened to overtake her.

Ullr raised his hand defensively. "Don't mind me, spitfire."

She turned back toward the Utførelse. The rune he etched onto her skin surged toward her eyes. It gave her the power to see clearly, to see across great distances—something a mortal could never be capable of.

As her vision grew sharp and near, Astrid focused on the prisoner being dragged into the Utførelse. Blonde hair, platinum on Asgard but looking dirtied anywhere else, was pulled into a loose tail down his back. The Asgardian armor he once wore no longer shielded his skin. Instead, he only wore flimsy trousers that were ripped and stained, the ice already impeding on his bare feet. The prisoner's chest had streaks of old wounds scattered across it, stray golden blood drying against his skin.

Thor.

Even then, after spending years together and seeing each other at their worst, the wind still caught in Astrid's throat. Shimmering gold blood dried along the prince's face, droplets of it scattering along his chest. He hung his head low, blonde curls framing either side of his face. The light cascaded off his skin like a kaleidoscope and displayed across the icy floor.

Thor's head shot up. Those sterling blue eyes landed on her instantly, as if he could hear her mind calling out to him.

"Looks like they gave him an extra beating," Astrid murmured, rubbing the magic out of her eyes. It had begun to sting unpleasantly.

Ullr chuckled. "Do you blame them?"

She turned and watched him with narrowed eyes. "Let's just get back to the mission." Scooching backward, Astrid yanked her bow back out, knocking one of the wooden arrows. "Stand fast, Ullr."

"Always the soldier," he teased.

Astrid exhaled.

Overcome your fear.

She pulled the bowstring. The tip hovered over the chieftain Jotunn once more. Below, the Jotunn chanted garish words as they circled Thor. Loud beats from drums echoed across the gorge. A few warrior Jotunn handed an extravagant greatsword to their chieftain. He raised it above his head as he shrieked a war cry through the air.

The mission was simple.

Prince Thor allowed the Jotunn to capture him on a raid gone wrong. They brought him back to their village and proceeded with a trial to execute him. *Trial* was a kind word. The Jotunn were geared and ready to remove the head of the famed Asgardian Prince long before the company ever stepped foot on Jotunheim.

Astrid's eyes glanced behind the chieftain, at the very top of his icy throne. An eight-sided jewel, colored a sterling white, glowed and radiated a humming energy at its spot upon the throne. The priceless artifact commonly known as Odin's Tear was lost to the Aesir clan ages ago. Finally, it was within their grasp, soon to be returned to its rightful home, within the All-Father's hands.

If I can shoot a damned arrow.

A distraction was all it took. If the Jotun's thought an invasion was underway, they'd scatter. They'd return to their icy caves in fear of the Aesir releasing their wrath upon them once more.

No distraction, no retreat.

"Astrid," Ullr suddenly said. "Loki's signaling again."

She caught the glimmer of light in the corner of her eye. It was frantic, desperate, *fearful.* Astrid was doing just what they thought she would do. Clamping up.

"Never mind it," she whispered.

The bow wobbled, but she held it firmly, pointing the arrowhead back toward the chieftain's crown. One arrow and she could knock it off his head. The Jotunn drew nearer to Thor, still proclaiming some speech to his people in a language Astrid didn't care to learn. It rattled her ears as the feathers lining the tail end of the arrow tickled her cheek.

Overcome your fear!

But then it hit her, and Astrid was no longer in the icy tundra of Jotunnheim.

Once, there might've been an archer in the same spot as her, the arrow point angled directly toward an unsuspecting village. Astrid remembered it as if it happened seconds ago.

Before the Royal Guard, before Thor, before missions beside gods, Astrid was merely a farmer who witnessed her village suffer a massacre at the hands of the ones she worshiped the most.

Astrid's eyes focused on Thor within the Utførelse.

The bow wavered.

Years ago, Thor's father led a stampede through Herjan, Astrid's home. It was a quiet village, one with retired warriors and large homesteads. They were merchants and farmers, travelers finding solace in rolling hills. A flowing river struck through Herjan and went all the way through the valley, around the golden city, beneath the castle.

To her, it was far grander than the castle itself.

To the Aesir gods of Asgard, it was where unsettling rumors brewed. Word of an uprising rippled through the town, slowly making its way to the golden castle itself. In return, the gods came to the village and silenced any hint of a rumor.

Silenced was a kind word for it.

Astrid blinked rapidly. A cold breeze brushed over the gorge, the arrow shaking and fumbling. She breathed in sharply, her fingers growing numb from the cold and barely holding onto the bowstring. Within the gorge, the ceremony continued, and the chieftain raised his sword over his head. The rune lingered behind her eyes, and her vision focused. In the blade's reflection, she saw the anger of a thousand gods within Thor's eyes.

"Astrid!"

She flinched and released the arrow.

Thwip!

The thin wooden shaft wobbled as it shot through the air, whistling as it soared down into the gorge. For a moment, relief washed through Astrid. She did it. She fired the arrow, she began the distraction, she saved Thor's life and pushed the mission forward.

"Bloody hell," Ullr whispered. "Astrid."

She followed his gaze. The arrow landed too far from where they gathered. It was barely noticed, barely heard over the rushing wind. In the distance, a blizzard quickly approached. Not a damned soul noticed it.

Astrid lowered her bow. "Oh, *fuck.*"

Everything happened all at once.

The chieftain was moments away from striking his blade down across Thor's neck. The prince, brimming with untamed anger, raised his head, thunder and lightning dancing around in his crystal eyes. Across the gorge, Astrid could barely make out Loki rising from his hiding spot, another figure—the sorceress—following at his feet.

"It's over," Ullr said. "We need to get down there before Thor does something we can't fix."

Astrid couldn't move. She felt frozen to the ground, staring down at the man she spent nights with, the man she woke up beside, the man she dreamt of and worshiped. She had failed, and the amount of his fury was something Astrid couldn't stop imagining.

Ullr snatched her. "Astrid! We need to go!"

But it was already happening.

The Prince of Asgard burst out of his restraints. He released a howling war cry, one that enveloped the air and shook the icy walls surrounding the gorge. The god did not carry a weapon, nor even don any armor, but he never once needed them. He rose to his feet like he was never a prisoner.

Most of the Jotunn within the Utførelse were merely villagers. There were women and children, pregnant giants with round, growing bellies. The warriors were mostly old, aged soldiers who no longer fought in true battles. Killing the Prince of Asgard was a ceremonial act, something they thought they deserved.

Perhaps...

She shook her head.

Astrid fell to the ground, desperate to have the snowy floor against her skin. The ice beneath her did not bring any comfort. There was only a chill, and it was paired with the sounds of terrified screams and spilled blood. Even from their distance, she heard limbs being ripped from the socket, blood splattering across the snow, souls fading up into the air.

"Another massacre," she whispered.

Ullr stood, looking down at her with an unreadable expression. "Another day."

TWO

Blood and ice.

That was all that was left. A handful of the Jotunn managed to run off, finding safety in their hidden caves that were uninhabitable for people like Astrid. Even her company of gods would suffer to live in such conditions. The jewel, Odin's Tear, no longer sat on its pedestal within the chieftain's throne. During the chaos, it had been taken and returned to its hiding spot.

Astrid crept through the abandoned Utførelse. The minuscule tents once lining the ceremonial space had smoke trailing up from them, holes seared through the sheen leather. Scorch marks, black and streaked with ash, were scattered across the gorge. Even stretching up the walls. The smoke lingered low in the air. The remaining heat singed Astrid's nose hairs as she drew nearer. It was a frightening parallel: an irreversible cold splattered with a heat strong enough to burn a body to ash.

Thor's mighty thunderbolt was not one to scoff at. It came out of nowhere, perhaps the very depths of his soul, and struck whoever dared to draw near. All that remained were piles of smoke and debris, the world forever scarred.

Astrid stepped over a severed limb.

Pools of the inky blue blood spread like rivers across the gorge. They stained Astrid's feet, splattering onto her aged golden armor. In the center, where Thor once sat as a prisoner of war, was a child. Astrid winced. There was an emphasis on the *was*.

Footsteps followed closely behind her.

"Three years."

Astrid stood in front of the throne, where the dead chieftain lay at her feet. His head was nowhere to be found, but the obsidian headdress he wore was cracked and shattered on the throne. Surprisingly, Jotunn bled like mortals, except for the deep blue tint their blood gave off. She turned to see the sorceress storming up to her.

"Sigyn," Astrid said in a warning tone, readying her weak defense. "The arrow—"

The sorceress raised her hand. Unlike the other gods, Sigyn did not bother to wrap herself with fur cloaks to withstand the cold. Her inherent power allowed her to have a fire smoldering beneath her skin, never once letting the chill reach her. She dressed in simple robes, her ebony skin glowing in the shockingly bright world. While she held a primary seat within the Aesir pantheon of gods and goddesses, Sigyn remained the most powerful and skilled sorceress in all the Nine Realms. Hundreds of students flocked to her halls in Asgard with a plethora of gifts meant to convince her to spare some knowledge.

Behind her, her godly husband, Loki, crept through the massacre.

"Give me one of your excuses," Sigyn hissed, "and I'll make sure you end up like the rest of them."

Loki came up behind her. "Dear one," he cooed, snaking an arm around her waist. "Have pity on our farmgirl." He glanced over Sigyn's head at Astrid, a teasing smirk pulling across his lips.

Astrid held his dark stare and glared. "I am not your farmgirl."

The trickster god was the eldest. Long black curls fell down his back, littered with a series of braids and jewels. The armor he wore, light and easy to move in, was colored black and purple, framed after the glow of his magic. His marriage to Sigyn occurred centuries ago, long before Astrid had ever come into being. They were an odd pairing, but perhaps that was the guarantee for success.

"I will *not* pity the one who ruined three years of work," Sigyn growled, her almond-shaped eyes never once leaving Astrid. "What you have done cannot be undone."

Astrid looked over her shoulder at the throne. "I know."

Ice cracked beneath their feet as Ullr hopped down from the top of the throne. "Not to change the subject," he mused, "but has anyone *seen* the big guy?"

A silence settled in on the company.

No one had seen him. The sounds of war overtook the gorge as both archers on either wall raced down to the village. It was a steep trek, and by the time they made it to the bottom, there was only an echo of a battle. Fallen soldiers took their final groans before collapsing against the ice. Scattered footprints littered the snow while the shouts of runaway Jotunn could be heard in the distance. But when they arrived, no one noticed Thor's absence.

Astrid glanced around. Ullr was the only one who dared to look nonchalant.

"Damned Prince," Loki snarled. The mischievous grin he wore only moments ago was clouded by sudden stress, something that Astrid was oddly familiar with.

At least, when it came to Thor, she was more than familiar with it.

Sigyn thrusted a finger at Astrid. "This is *your* fault, farmer girl."

"I am not a farmer girl!" She snapped back, raising her bow. "I've earned my place in this company, as much as the rest of you!"

The sorceress bit back a bitter laugh. "You mean, you *pleased* the Crowned Prince of Asgard enough to convince his father of letting a"—Sigyn reached, her slender and long fingers tugging at Astrid's golden Royal Guard armor— "weak-willed mortal who needs petty armor for protection along an expedition with gods." Her smirk was wicked, sharp, and cruel. "Does that just about sum it up, *farmer girl*?"

Astrid's hands clenched into tight fists as a rush of familiar heat burst across her cheeks and seeped down beneath the armor she wore. She didn't need a mirror to know that blotchy red patches began to sprout against her skin. When she was only a girl, her mother used to retrieve her Viking helm from the wall, grasping it by the horns and resting it upon Astrid's small head. The helmet sank lower than it should've.

"It's your *krigerblod*[1] showing, Astrid," her mother teased. "Do not hide your anger or trap it beneath your skin." She would pinch the red spots that littered Astrid's face. "You have warrior blood. Let it breathe."

Astrid raised her face to Sigyn, who stood at least a head taller than her. "I am descended from warriors," she snarled as she widened her stance. "I have earned my place beside you."

"Since when is failure considered worthy of a place beside the gods?"

Astrid's hand hovered over the blade at her hip. Sigyn was a being beyond her power, beyond her age, beyond anything Astrid ever imagined. Sigyn knew existence before Astrid ever did, before she was ever a glimpse in her mother's mind.

But then, she imagined holding her blade beneath the sorceress's neck, watching the golden blood trickle down the edge and onto her skin. The divinity, like a drug, would seep into her. For a moment, the shortest of seconds, immortality would grab hold of her, and Astrid would snatch it up with her greedy human fingers. She was seconds away from carelessly retrieving her blade.

"*Stille*[2]!" Loki hissed. "Do you hear that?"

Astrid took a step away from the sorceress. Shouting echoed in the distance. It rang familiar, deep, and angry. Her eyes widened. "Thor," she whispered. "It's him."

---

1. Translation: Warrior blood.

2. Translation: Quiet!

"That damned idiot," Loki snapped. "He'll pull the entire realm into a war before the day is even over." He shouldered his pack, reaching for his wife's hand. "Let's go."

Before he ran, Loki's eyes landed on Astrid. A million words rested behind his eyes.

Why must you love him?

Why can't you hate him?

And finally, *I am ashamed of you.*

They were the same words he always said when he looked at her, even without opening his mouth. Astrid looked away. She was in no mood to hear his complaints any longer.

The bond she had with Thor was something more than taboo. It was forbidden, a hated idea to any being with golden blood. Thor tainted himself by touching Astrid, by allowing her to remain so close to his side. Just as much as his divinity seeped into her, the mortality she carried like a disease clung effortlessly to him.

"Aren't you comin', love?"

Astrid met Ullr's stare. Loki and Sigyn were already running toward the echoing screams.

"Are you ashamed of me, Ullr?" she suddenly asked.

He frowned and hesitated, taking a step backward. "The big man needs you."

"No god needs me."

Ullr sighed before storming up to her. He snatched her chin, ashen fingers digging into her skin and forcing her to hold his stare.

"You let that sorceress get under your skin, and you'll never have a backbone."

"And yet," she whispered, "you cannot answer the question."

He furrowed his brow and released her. "We ought to go before we lose the company in the blizzard."

Ullr started running, and Astrid felt herself following.

THREE

Jotunnheim had a resounding silence to it.

Despite the oncoming storm, the wind that swept the snow into the air and shot it past Astrid's cheeks like daggers, there was hardly a sound. The brewing weather rested on the horizon, for now, but slowly gained speed, inching closer and closer to where the Jotunn's lived. Their caves blocked most of the storm, the entrances pressing deep into the ground below and within the permanent ice.

Astrid grew up knowing that it was foolish—it was *worse* than foolish—to set foot in one of the Jotunn's caves. If the world outside of them was cold, within their hideouts was drastically different, a temperature dipping below what the strongest god could handle.

Beneath their feet, ice cracked and creaked. In the distance, shrouded slightly by the snowy mist, Astrid saw the rest of the company, their arms raised to combat the weather. Beyond them were the very caves she dreaded, where the Jotunn went and hid away after Thor broke free and attacked.

Shouts began to echo across the plain.

Astrid held her breath. Thor stood in front of the tallest cave entrance she had ever seen. It reached high into the sky above, a wide opening stretching into a deep blue darkness. The color was the same as the untouched oceans or the unmanned night skies. For a moment, Astrid was entranced by it, almost staggering forward and letting herself step within it. But the rest of her company stood starkly in front of her, not daring to venture closer than they needed to.

If there was one thing the gods feared, it was their Jotunn brethren.

Astrid crept closer, stepping around Ullr to get a better look at Thor.

The missing chieftain's head dangled from his hand.

"Odin's breath," Loki murmured, his eyes growing wide as he neared the prince. "Thor!" He shot forward, ignoring Sigyn's tight grip over his elbow. Grasping Thor's shoulder, the trickster god tried to yank him back, but it was to no avail.

Thor was one of the youngest gods in the Aesir clan, making him reckless, making him volatile. Making him stronger than his aged family.

"Stop this, Thor," Loki said in his ear. "Before you bring the wrath of your father to Jotunnheim's doorstep!"

Thor tilted his head, and Astrid caught a glimpse of his piercing blue eyes, tinted silver from the remnants of lightning within him. A smirk tugged across his face as he jerked his arm back, shoving Loki toward the rest of the company.

"My father isn't here," Thor snarled over his shoulder. Turning back to the echoing cave opening, a gust of air rushing out to meet them, Thor began to raise the severed head up. "*Jotunns!*"

Deep blue blood trickled down onto the snow silently.

"Bring out what belongs to me," he demanded as he rolled the chieftain's head into the cave. "Or all of Jotunnheim will meet your leader's fate!"

The world went still around them. Not even wind curled out of the cave. Astrid reached for her bow, retrieving another thin arrow from her quiver.

"Don't—!" Loki's hand snapped toward her, his head shaking rapidly. "This was a retrieval mission! We are not meant to take life!"

She hesitated, almost slipping the arrow back from where it came, but the prince's unwavering presence forced her morals into a corner.

Thor laughed but the sound lacked any humor. "Do not stop my shadow, Loki."

My shadow.

The cold reached Astrid suddenly, and a chill rolled down her spine. But without even thinking, she kept arming herself.

Loki was no longer backing down, storming toward the prince once more. "You have overstepped your—"

"*Koh!*"

Astrid's head snapped up. "What was that?"

"*Rah!*"

Thundering footsteps echoed from deep within the cave. Icy cold wind rushed forward, shoving the gods and Astrid back a step or two. She clutched her bow to her chest.

"Dah!"

Sigyn clapped her hands together, a puff of energy exhaling from her palms. A language Astrid did not recognize left Sigyn's lip in quiet murmurs as her limbs began to glow with an otherworldly power. Tendrils grew from her palms, curling around her body till there were whips lying in her hands. They trailed against the ground despite being a magical object created out of thin air. It was an ability unique to Sigyn, one she built and crafted over her divine life. The silvery magic grew weapons that were as sharp as the deadliest blade, capable of doing more harm than it seemed.

Skyggemagi[1] was what the Asgardians called it.

"The Jotunns!" Sigyn shouted. "It's a battle chant!"

From the center of the cave, a single figure began to take shape. Taller than any god, with aquatic colored skin, was a Jotunn. Starkly white antlers protruded from the top of the creature's head, almost reaching the top of the cave's entrance. It wielded a singular axe, the silver blade shimmering when the light splashed against it.

Thor remained still and Astrid could only imagine the smile that graced his lips.

Astrid flipped her bow out in front of her, knocking the arrow on the string and pulling it to the curve of her cheek. The string

---

1. Translation: Shadow magic.

pressed into her skin, surely leaving a mark, but she hardly cared. Her eyes focused on the prince before latching onto the Jotunn, the arrow releasing before she had a chance to breathe.

The arrow whipped through the air.

Thunk!

It sank into the Jotunn's chest, and the creature staggered backwards before collapsing, pale blue knees thudding against the ice beneath their feet.

Thor laughed and held his arms out to either side of him. "*That is my warrior!*" He held his hand out. "Weapon, Ullr!"

Like an obedient dog, Ullr retrieved a blade from his belt, twisting the handle around for Thor to take. The prince snatched it from him, pressing another hand to his chest as he faced Astrid.

Astrid replicated the stance, her heart stammering beneath her fist. To understand her connection to Thor would mean to pry the skin from her flesh and stare into the soul beneath. Astrid hardly understood it herself, and she didn't quite want to know it all the same. Even then, when Thor was moments away from being attacked by the Jotunn, Astrid managed to do the one thing that rendered her incapable of completing their mission.

Firing the arrow.

Taking a life.

Beside her, Loki's glare practically seared into the side of her face. "Do you know what you have done?"

"There's hardly time to discuss it," Sigyn snapped, her eyes widening at the cave's entrance. "More approach! Arm yourselves!"

As if they all shared a single heartbeat, the company stepped in time with each other. Astrid rushed forward, pulling another arrow from her quiver before standing beside Thor, aiming at the next Jotunn who shot toward them. Ullr, an archery master, produced his bow beside her, the runes beneath his clothes glowing ominously.

"Forgive me," Loki muttered as he produced his staff, Laevateinn, from thin air. The sleek weapon forged from obsidian and priceless jewels was fashioned by Loki's own hand. Within the scepter's tip, a crystal burned bright like an amethyst, channeling his power.

Floods of Jotunn began to burst through the cave's mouth. They screamed and bellowed their garish words, sounding more like a frightening symphony than a slew of chants. The company was fractured instantly, being pulled every which way to fight off the giants. Astrid rolled through the snow, raising her bow above her head and firing a chain of arrows toward an approaching giant's belly. The beast let out a hollow of pain before collapsing into the ice, the world cracking beneath their feet.

Behind her, Sigyn's magic slid across the air, slicing through the Jotunns' skin as though they were made from nothing at all. Loki disappeared and reappeared in different spots around her, never staying in the same place for one second.

Astrid started to raise herself back up and rejoin the battle.

"*No!*" The Jotunn warrior's hand shot forward and snatched her ankle.

The ice cracked further beneath the Jotunn's weight. An ocean world, one that stretched as far as time itself, lived under the ice of Jotunnheim. While the gods feared the Jotunn themselves, the sea below was unknown to all and feared by even more.

Astrid clawed at the snow, desperately kicking her feet but unable to sever the giant's tight grip over her leg. Her eyes snapped up, focusing on the rest of her company battling off the army of Jotunn. There was an unmistakable glow surrounding each of the gods, like a golden halo. The power wafted off them in waves, forcing back the Jotunn effortlessly. Astrid watched them like a child being torn from her family, the mortality holding onto her as tightly as the Jotunn.

Tears struck down her face before she had the chance to realize they were there. The breath came out of her in gasps and pants as she dragged her hands through the snow, the screams slipping from her next. The ice concaved beneath her and the Jotunn, moments away from swallowing them both whole.

Astrid's life danced before her eyes, and she met it with shame. She could see Thor in the dance, his skin covered in blood and gore, eyes wild with adrenaline, not a care on his face. She reached for him, but it was no use.

The ice shuddered beneath her, and Astrid tipped into the sea, the freezing water nipping at her feet for a split second.

Loki materialized in front of her, a purple trail of magic curling around his shoulders. He reached, grabbing her by the elbows and hoisting her out of the water below. The Jotunn sank into the sea and disappeared within the inky darkness.

"Once," Loki whispered in her ear, "there was a farmer girl who plowed the fields and waited for her father's return."

Astrid hated how she clutched to his armor, but there was a wobble in her legs, and she was doubting her ability to stand upright. "Shut up," she hissed, swatting at him like a fly.

"That isn't any way to thank the man who saved you, is it?"

Shoving herself off his chest, Astrid pushed herself forward, ignoring the fear that still clung to her. Immediately, she saw Thor a few yards away, the battle fresh on his face, a wild excitement dancing across his fingers like lightning bolts. There was a Jotunn in front of him, but the beast barely stood a chance. Thor moved like a viper, striking and biting mercilessly

A few final warriors met their ends at Sigyn's whip, the silverly magic latching around limbs and tightening until they snapped off. Whatever army remained sank deeper into the hole the Jotunn's lived in. They would not creep out into the light for days, Astrid assumed.

The snowy ground was littered with Jotunn bodies and pools of blue blood. A strangely uncomfortable smell settled in the air, one that caused Astrid's empty stomach to swirl and bubble. She staggered, not entirely regaining feeling in her shaking legs. Purple mist, Loki's calling card, peered through her peripheral.

Loki reanimated on her left, walking in time with her. "This farmer girl," he continued playfully, his voice mocking and high-pitched, "is forced to live amongst the stars, and soon forgets..." Loki stopped, sliding over to stand directly in front of her, his charismatic face suddenly dreadfully serious. "That she is *not* one."

"What a nice thing to say," Astrid snapped.

"Don't be like that." Loki stepped closer, his shadow draping across her, though she wasn't that much shorter. "The prince is teetering on a line I am afraid I cannot pull him away from. Perhaps you might." He leaned forward. "But you won't get very far by feeding into it."

Astrid glared at him. "If you have a problem, handle it yourself."

His thick brow furrowed as he stared, his jaw tight and tense. "Fine," he grumbled. "Watch me handle it myself, Astrid."

The god disappeared in the blink of an eye, reappearing closer to the rest of the company. Gathering up a deep breath, Astrid walked the distance to join them, though there was a voice in the back of her head telling her to run in the opposite direction. Now that the fighting was settled, there was the matter of the mission to discuss, and it all led back to Astrid.

"Tell me," Thor said as they all reconvened, his gaze looking down at the bodies surrounding him, "who failed to do what they were meant to? Back at the gorge?"

An uneasy silence spread between them.

Astrid swallowed, her heart pattering like a bird trapped beneath her skin. Below her, for the second time that day, her legs shook and trembled. When was the last time she felt such fear? Astrid could hardly pinpoint a certain time, but the moment Thor's steely gaze fell onto her, there was nothing else for her to think about. There was only the thunder god and his growing rage.

She breathed in again. *How could he hurt me?* Astrid nodded to herself. *He could never hurt me.*

Astrid opened her mouth to speak.

"Was my aim not true, my Prince?" Loki cooed as he stepped forward. There was a familiarly playful glimmer in his eyes, one that pulled a smile from even his stoic sorceress wife. It was effortless for him to lighten the mood, to bring an ease back where it belonged.

But, in that moment, Astrid knew that Loki meant to take the blame for her mistake, and it drove her further into an irreversible fear.

Thor's hand tightened around the hilt of his sword. "Do you regard my orders as a game?"

"Oh, by Odin's beard!" Loki put his hands on his hips, a smirk pulling across his face. "Did you *mean* for me to take it seriously?" He laughed lightly with a shake of his head. "Well, now, all this time, I—"

Thunder clapped through the silence, and Thor was suddenly upon him, staring the trickster god in the face. "I hold you in no different regard than I do these Jotunn, old man," he hissed.

Astrid's eyes widened. Sparks of lightning streaked out from the prince's eyes. She stepped closer, reaching a cautious hand toward him.

"You cannot kill me," Loki whispered. "Your father—"

Thor pulled his blade back up, holding it beneath Loki's neck. He reached to grab the god by the hair, to press the edge of the sword further against his throat. The others were frozen in place, the fear etched across their faces.

Thor the Boulder, moments away from slaughtering an ancient creature, born before time itself.

No. Astrid was plagued, suddenly, with the words Loki had said to her, how he whispered them into her ear. *Once, there was a farmer girl who plowed the fields and waited for her father's return.* She rushed forward.

Grasping onto Thor's arm, Astrid yanked him back, stepping up to speak in his ear. "Spare him," she whispered, "my love."

The prince turned, ever so slightly. "What for?"

"You know why."

"Suppose I don't," he whispered. Those crystal eyes snapped over to her. "Convince me."

For someone who claimed to be delivering orders and not playing a game, Thor amused himself through Astrid's never-ending loyalty. Perhaps he'd never whisper the words aloud, but he knew it as much as she did. The rope that bound them together was one they both held, tugging and pulling till the other lost their grasp.

Astrid's eyes snapped toward Loki. He hardly looked afraid, a smirk tugging at his lip. That was the fickle thing with gods. Indestructible and fragile at the same time. Thor was the Prince of the Aesir, the future of Asgard, the pride of his father. Ready to risk it all for the mere crime of wounding his pride, his ego. Astrid knew it all too well. To satisfy him, she needed to think like a god.

"Kill him," she said, and Thor raised a surprised brow. "And face the wrath of the All-Father."

He looked away, unimpressed. The blade's edge pressed against Loki's throat, plucking strands of dark hair.

"*Now* is not the time for the trickster's death!"

Thor hesitated, a glimmer in his eye. "Now?"

"Do you not wish to outdo him? Let all of Asgard see the impurities of the god they wish to hold in such high regard?"

The words hung in the air. Thor watched her closely till a smile tugged across his face. Letting out a burly laugh, the blade lowered from beneath Loki's neck, falling to Thor's side as if he never threatened to wield it in the first place.

Loki's ebony eyes snapped toward Astrid. The anger within them was unbeatable.

With an untimely ease, Thor strode toward her with a lazy grin. He reached, dragging coarse fingertips through the streaks of icy blue blood across her cheek. The grin grew into something flirtatious, something that made Astrid want to cower from all the eyes that were angled in her direction.

"Look at you," Thor murmured. "Such a pretty little thing, with blood all over your face."

He passed by her.

Gulping down her rising shame, Astrid lifted her head toward the rest of her company. Despite being gods, they all wore exhaustion across their faces, looking over the mess they had made within Jotunnheim. A land that had not seen bloodshed for quite some time was faced with a massacre, a new wound that would remain starkly across their minds for much longer than any of the company realized.

Astrid tried to tell herself it wasn't her fault, though something told her that it was.

One by one, the remaining gods began to follow in Thor's footsteps. Sigyn let her shoulder smack into Astrid as she passed her, not caring enough to soften the blow of her agitation. In the end, there was only Loki, still standing in the spot where Thor had almost killed him. He stared into the snow, his teeth clenched so hard it made his jaw go rigid.

Once, they were friends.

Astrid used to cling to the edge of Loki's cloak as he led her through the tall hallways of Asgard's golden castle. Each night, he led her through the darkness, all the way to Thor's chambers. She would slip inside, and Loki would leave, ready to make the trek the next night and then the next. Her mouth opened as snow began to fall from the sky.

All the things she wished to say ran amok in her head: *I know what I say, but I am not cruel. I swear.*

I am kind, somewhere.

There is love within me. Somewhere.

Loki stormed by her, the words left unsaid.

FOUR

Astrid tended not to think about the day she met Thor.

There was nothing romantic about it. One day, she was homeless, living off Asgard's streets, trying to survive after a massacre. The next, she had a cot within the barracks, training to become a member of the Royal Guard, an army that served the All-Father, made up of mortal Asgardians. Ullr, who used to be the figurehead of the army, led a battle against a rival king, a Vanir god that sought to claim the Bleeding Throne of Asgard as his own. The Aesir pantheon found their greatest enemies in their other halves, the second pantheon – the Vanir – within the Nine Realms that had been expelled from Asgard long ago.

Astrid hardly remembered the war itself. There was a moment where she rested at Ullr's side, overlooking the quiet field and witnessing a view of death that was not meant for any mortal. She saw what the Valkyrie witnessed before plucking the souls of perished soldiers for Valhalla. She looked over a battlefield, saw the low-hanging stench of death and growing smog.

It was not until afterward, when the fighting had been set and done that Astrid first truly spoke to the Prince of Asgard.

They took up camp a few miles away from the battlefield, but the smell of war remained. A long tent was erected within their encampment, makeshift tables full of roasted animals and tankards full of mead lining the space. Astrid drank her fourth mug of mead, feeling the fruity concoction begin to swirl through her stomach unpleasantly. She swayed around the wooden table, slipping in and around the joyous soldiers. They celebrated their victory, mocked the dead, and played with the wounded. Prisoners from the rival army danced above a fire, rope tied to the tent's ceiling keeping them afloat.

Astrid barely paid mind to any of it. She stumbled toward the front, where a few taller seats had been hoisted onto a makeshift stage. They were for the gods, to separate them from their lesser mortal soldiers. Ullr leaned against the back of his seat, holding a mug lazily in one hand while looking over a tattered map. Beside him, moving little emblems around the map, was Prince Thor.

Back then, his hair curled around his ears boyishly, a gentle curve lining his cheeks.

"We will march for the golden city at dawn," the prince commanded.

In her drunken state, Astrid only paid attention to the shimmering halo that encircled him. It pulsed and grew with every step she took, his divinity coaxing her forward with a gentle tug. Perhaps Astrid had always been addicted to the power, long before she ever had her first taste of it. Or maybe it was the mead.

Astrid stumbled until she knocked into the prince from behind. His divinity sent a shiver down her spine.

Ullr glanced in her direction, his lip tugging up in amusement. "Other way, soldier," he said, nodding his chin in the opposite direction.

"We need a fight," Astrid blurted. She didn't quite understand herself at first, though her voice clapped against the walls of the tent, calling the attention of more Asgardians. "A brawl," she repeated.

The prince kept his back to her, only angling his chin above his shoulder. Sterling grey eyes sliced into her. His brow arched, the boyish look he carried rendered unseen by his unimaginable power. He chuckled in amusement before looking back at his map, ignoring her presence.

"Ullr," he snapped. "Pay attention."

The war god eyed Astrid closely, shaking his head. *Step back. Turn around.*

Astrid happened to be quite tired of stepping back. Of turning around.

Still swaying with an unavoidable drunkenness, Astrid reached behind her, ripping an axe from another soldier's belt. Astrid swung the double-bladed axe forward, aiming for the prince's armored shoulder.

What was she thinking? How could she be so foolish?

But Astrid was deep within a haze, remembering all that she had lost, remembering all that she had taken. Perhaps the prince would give her an easy death. Perhaps the Vikings would sing and write stories about her.

She wanted the pain, and the god with blonde hair and blue eyes could give it to her.

The prince moved in the blink of an eye. He stood only a foot away, his gloved hand catching the blade in the air. "Well, well," he cooed, his voice deep and gravely. "A *kriger*[1] with a death wish."

Astrid ripped the axe back and stumbled. The soldiers surrounding her inched away. They did not watch her like a traitor, but rather with amusement, as if she might be their real entertainment, their reward for winning.

"Thor," Ullr shouted, his hands clenched. "L-Let the girl be. She's just drunk."

The prince shook his head. "She asked for a fight. Who am I to deny her?"

Astrid's heart hammered as he retrieved his spear. The weapon moved like an extension of his arm, slicing and swiping through the air with a deadly sound behind it. Astrid danced around like a snake, ducking and weaving with every thrust he made. The axe felt loose and detached in her hands. The spear sank forward again, the tip slicing her cheek.

Red blood dribbled down her chin and splashed against the ground. Astrid grasped onto her face, but the god was upon her in an instant, knocking the axe out of her hand. Thor snatched onto her chin, his fingers digging into her skin.

Thor's eyes dragged over her face, his lip tugging up. "Why do you wish for death, *kriger*?"

---

1. Translation: Warrior.

"I do not—"

"Then fight back." He released her with a shove, kicking the axe back to her. "Go on!" Thor's eyes were wild and alight with lightning. "Strike your god!"

The battle cry was hurled out the back of Astrid's throat before she realized what she was doing. She snatched up the axe and shot forward, holding it high above her head before slamming it down upon him. Thor deflected with his spear, a brilliantly sharp laugh shrieking through the air. Astrid felt like an untamed berserker, suddenly full of a power she was unable to carry within her mortal skin. The axe whistled as it flew above her head and down upon him, again and again.

Thor never once stopped laughing or dodging, drunk on the battle.

It wasn't until the edge of the axe slid against Thor's neck, slicing through his immortal skin and producing a thin line of golden blood, that the brawl changed into something else entirely.

Astrid swayed as the blood caught onto her skin, sinking into her like an elixir. The divinity coursed into her almost instantly. The axe fell from her hand and clattered against the ground. She had never felt something so sweet, something so cruel, something so dangerous. Euphoria and fear danced within Astrid's stomach as she became drunk on Thor's divinity.

Shink!

Thor's spear collided into her shoulder, the tip sinking through her skin as though she were made of nothing. As quickly as the divinity found her, it sank away, leaving her to be a desperate mortal, begging for more. She couldn't even feel the pain, couldn't even notice her legs giving out beneath her, the world swaying all around her.

Astrid came back to her senses hours later. She lay outside, the moon high above her head. A cool breeze slipped through her hair, down her body, through the thin clothes she wore. Her armor was gone, somewhere else. The wound upon her shoulder was gone, some sort of healing concoction already used. Astrid pushed herself forward, missing the haze the mead had once given her.

"Tell me why."

She flinched at the deep voice behind her. The Prince of Asgard sat against the ash-covered floor, staring out over the smoky battlefield that his army had left behind. There was no crown upon his head, no armor covering his body.

Astrid gulped. She raised a blade against her Prince, against the future ruler of Asgard, against the one she was meant to bend the knee to. "Why, what?" was all she managed to choke out.

"Why have you named me to be your executioner?"

"I never claimed to ask for death."

Thor's lip twitched. "Perhaps." He angled himself toward her, those eyes finding her and not daring to let go. There was something twisted about Asgard's Prince, a rumor that hung over his head like a storm cloud. All the people knew of it, though none dared to ever speak it aloud. A cruelty lived within Thor, as if something had rotted within him before he was born. Despite that, Astrid looked upon him and saw only a man. She shook her head. *It is the divinity lingering within your eyes.*

Thor remained silent as he watched her, something heavy lingering within his gaze. Astrid felt like a ghost, like her entire self was see-through, and he could peer into her soul without asking. He could see the darkness before she let it out, the truth she desperately tried to keep inside. Astrid *did* want the god to kill her, to end the loneliness that plagued her. Thor's mouth stretched into a wicked smirk as he stared relentlessly, his brow arching.

"Why do you watch me like that?"

Thor tilted his head. "Like what, little *kriger*?"

She bristled, the name he gave her sending a swirl of feelings through her body, ones that she was in no hurry to acknowledge. "As if you are a predator," Astrid said, "and have finally found your prey."

That smirk widened. "Does that please you?"

"N-No!" Astrid glared as a burning hot sensation surged toward her cheeks. "You—"

"Then why does your heart hammer like a hummingbird?"

"Because," she breathed as he inched closer to her, "You are my god. I am meant to—" The words hitched in the back of her throat, his presence unbearable.

"You are meant to *what*?" There was too much pleasure on his face.

"To worship you."

Thor chuckled. "Tell me, do you worship your gods, little *kriger*?"

Astrid knew, somehow, that she had one foot stuck in an irreversible future. Darkness beckoned her forward, a feeling unlike what currently plagued her beginning to sink into her skin. Perhaps it was not the right path to follow, perhaps it was more dooming than before. But Astrid found herself leaning toward the thunder god, caught in a trance she was incapable of escaping. A piece of her wished to ask why, to know what it was about her that drew his attention in her direction. Why hadn't he killed her in the tent? Why didn't he banish her for her disrespect?

What was a mortal to a god?

Before she could speak again, Thor let out a sigh and rose to his feet. Behind him, the celebration continued in the tent.

"You are free to go, little *kriger*."

Astrid's eyes went wide. "I'm...*what*?"

"If freedom is what you wish for," Thor said, "it is yours to take. There are Nine Realms at your disposal. You may never get another chance." His brow arched sharply. "Will you take it?"

"I don't understand," she murmured. "Fleeing the Royal Guard is considered treason."

Thor shrugged. "It is. Bar this one time. Like I said: you might never get another chance."

Perhaps it was the hopeful glimmer in her eyes that made him speak again.

"Stay," he said, his voice deep and shrouded by a snarl, "and I might never let you leave. Is that a risk you are willing to take?"

Astrid stared up at him, her jaw hanging open. There was amusement in his gaze, and something else—something primal and frightening. Her heart continued to slam relentlessly within her, not entirely from fear, but dipping into an odd sense of excitement. A deadly sort of thrill.

Astrid whispered, "Is my life a game to you?"

"I am a god, little *kriger*. I have to find excitement somewhere, don't I?"

Astrid was unsure of what it was that convinced her. She could hardly remember the last time she felt something, anything at all. There was only her blade and war, and blood. There were the memories, the fractured images fading in and out behind her eyes, recalling a massacre she might never forget. But then, there was the Asgardian Prince, and Astrid was alight with something she feared she might've never had the chance to have again.

And, in that moment, Astrid could've sworn she saw a flicker of humanity within Thor's steely gaze.

So, she stayed.

FIVE

"I miss the longhouses. The mead. The warmth of a fire in my belly."

The company walked on top of a frozen lake, miles of impenetrable ice striking down beneath their feet. The caves of the Jotunn were far behind, the bodies and pools of midnight colored blood remaining like a wound across the land.

In all the Nine Realms lay an oddly similar tree. It was wiry and old and decayed, with long arms that reached out in every direction. Leaves did not grow upon it; the roots did not stretch out anymore. It was a piece of Yggdrasil, the world tree, binding the realms together. Though it looked particularly dead in Jotunnheim, it was capable of opening portals to wherever the caster wished to go. It was how they arrived, and it was the only way they could leave.

As they walked, Astrid glanced down at her feet. The icy terrain of Jotunnheim simmered down slightly the closer they came to the tree. She imagined it to be the "end" of the realm, a spot that had one foot in the cosmos and another flat against the ground. Perhaps it was the only way a mortal could understand it, though she still had the incredibly uncomfortable sensation of lacking enough air to breathe the closer they came.

Random patches of greying grass, not entirely alive but not quite dead either, sprouted from within the snow. It no longer fell where they were, though when it did, Astrid tried to catch the flakes in the palm of her hand. The flake would melt against her skin, leaving small beads of icy crystals. She felt a few land against her head and reached for the next to fall.

Ullr held his hands behind his neck from in front of her; his pale face angled toward the cloudy sky. "And Jord's singing, of course."

A laugh scattered throughout the company, though none of them were as lighthearted as the archer god. Astrid held her bow tightly at her side, walking within the throng of four gods. Their divinity radiated off them like the sun, pouring an untamable heat onto her skin. Astrid greedily soaked it up, unable to handle the cold like her companions could.

"Don't lie," Loki called out from the rear. "*No one* enjoys Jord's singing."

At the front of the party, Thor walked alone. Astrid's eyes held onto him while the others reminisced, unable to feel the same sort of homesickness they reveled in. The kingdom they returned to expected Odin's Tear to be with them. The Aesir demanded that their traveling company of warriors be successful, to bring glory to the realm. Thor, as their inherent leader, would carry the burden of their failure. Astrid watched him and sank into her guilt.

Sigyn ran ahead as the tree came into view, her cloaks flying behind her elegantly. She slipped around Thor and pressed her bare palms against the ashy bark, her lips moving as incoherent whispers filled the air. The sorceress's eyes began to glow silver, ominous and powerful. More grass spiked up around the trees base.

"The portal home awaits us," she called out to the party.

Thor dropped his pack on the ground. "How long?"

"Minutes."

Astrid pressed forward and slid her bow into its quiver. Behind her, Loki approached with his arms twisted behind his back. She glanced at him sideways and gulped, focusing her attention on the ice cracking beneath her feet. The moment they returned, the Aesir would gather for an Althing, expecting to hear every detail from their journey. Down to the very moment when Astrid failed to complete her simple mission. Loki might've taken Thor's wrath, but the Aesir were not the same. The king, the All-Father, the One-Eyed Raven...he was not the same.

She opened her mouth to speak, but the trickster god was far quicker.

"Some days," Loki said in a quiet voice, "I wish I knew you before you were entangled with the Boulder."

Astrid's eyes fell upon Thor, who stood in front of the tree. "Why do you assume I was any different?"

"Don't make me laugh."

She eyed him, unable to stop her own smile, and elbowed his side. "Loki," Astrid murmured.

He smirked, though there was a softness behind it. Something gentle, but uneasy. "There is a sense of foreboding clouding my vision."

Astrid faced him with a raised brow. "Have the Norn blessed you with a glimpse into our future?"

"Never call it a blessing, Astrid." Loki's lip tugged down into a hard line. "They have shown me nothing but left a feeling upon my soul. A cut"—he paused, dragging one finger across his torso, from the tip of his sternum down to his belly— "across my being. Something approaches."

"Why are you telling me this?"

His ebony eyes fell upon her with an intensity that burned into her chest, unavoidable and pungent. "I believe it has to do with you, my little farmer girl."

Though the pet name normally riled her, Astrid became content beneath his stare. Somehow, Loki saw her as the person she once was, a figure she could not even see when she peered into a looking glass. If he could see it, it had to have been there.

Astrid pressed her lips together. "I don't—"

"*Helvete*[1] *!*" An invisible force shoved Sigyn backwards, her feet skidding against the icy floor below. With how close they were to the tree, the once frozen lake beneath their feet melted slightly, cracking heavily as they gathered. She gritted her teeth as she thrusted a hand toward the tree. "The portal will not open to me!"

---

1. Translation: Damn!

The company raced forward. The pale white tree creaked and moaned, the branches swaying despite the absence of wind. The center of the tree began to pull apart. The bark spread open in front of their eyes, a foggy mirror-like reflection beginning to appear within the middle of the tree.

"Is that not the portal?" Loki shouted.

Sigyn shook her head. "It is not mine!"

One by one, the members of the company retrieved their weapons and faced the growing hole in the tree. Sigyn's portals looked rather similar to it, but there was another force behind it, one none of them were expecting.

A figure began to take shape in the center of the tree. With silver hair and sharp, amethyst colored eyes, Astrid almost sank to her knees.

The Aesir god of law and order, Tyr.

Tyr was one that many Asgardians adored. He stood alongside Odin for centuries, acting as his noble advisor and closest friend. Most admired his unnatural beauty, hardly able to look away, even if they wanted to. And his voice was one of steel, powerful and bright. Even though they were realms apart from him, Tyr's power was not diminished in the slightest. He eyed the company warily, though his gaze did not linger on Astrid long enough for him to know she was there.

"Lord Tyr," Thor said, a breath of relief falling out of his godly companions. "We were just—"

"Moments away from returning home, I presume?" Tyr's voice echoed out of the tree and resounded through the quiet icy terrain of Jotunnheim. Despite not being in the realm, Tyr's slender and angular face held an obvious air of disgust about it. He raised a thin brow as he overlooked the company, perhaps looking for Odin's Tear. "I am afraid to inform you all that it is not time for your return. Not yet."

Thor stepped closer. "What has happened?"

"The All-Father has uncovered a weapon that will turn the tides of the Nine Realms. He who wields it controls the future of Asgard." Tyr leaned forward, almost inching through the portal and pressing into Jotunnheim. "And the Aesir demand it, before the Vanir catch wind of it."

Loki reached for his wife, tucking a hand around her waist and holding her close as a chill rose. It was an inherent movement, one that beckoned, one that spoke without uttering a single word. Astrid watched the exchange and had a sour taste in her mouth. She wished to spit on the ground, perhaps at Thor's feet. She shook her head. The cold grabbed hold of her easily.

"What sort of weapon is out there that we haven't already retrieved?" Loki asked.

"Better yet," Ullr muttered from Astrid's left, "one that we haven't already *made* ourselves."

She pressed her lips together, stifling a laugh.

"It comes from Svartalfheim." Tyr tilted his head. "The Dwarven realm."

Astrid knew little about those reclusive creatures. That is, she didn't know more than the average Asgardian.

"The land is riddled with labyrinths, isn't it?" she asked, her voice quiet. She spoke out of the corner of her mouth to Ullr. "Ask him for me, won't you?"

Ullr smirked and chuckled. "Lord Tyr"—he raised a hand politely, though Astrid knew he was teasing— "Svartalfheim is made up of labyrinths, correct?"

"Of course!" Tyr's brow furrowed quizzically. "You know that, Ullr!"

The archer god shot her a glare, his lip tugging into a smirk. "Got me in trouble," he mumbled.

Astrid shook her head, holding back her laugh once more. Out of all the Aesir, Tyr took the divide between mortal and divine rather seriously. The mundane were disregarded and ignored, where they belonged, Astrid assumed. Her involvement with the company merely came from Thor's insistence, something she didn't like to remind herself of. If it were up to Lord Tyr, Astrid would have never left her barracks and began to journey alongside the company of gods.

"Svartalfheim has grown since we last involved ourselves within it," Lord Tyr explained. "The Dwarf, Ivaldi, finds himself in a position of power these days."

Ullr leaned down and whispered in Astrid's ear. "Ivaldi, the master blacksmith. He controls the labyrinths and the miners."

"What does a tinkerer have to do with leading a realm?" Thor scoffed.

"It is the weapon he created, my Prince, that has given him such power." Tyr waved his hand through the reflection he spoke through, his portrait fading away to materialize into a hammer. The handle was wrapped with midnight colored leather, tightly wound over priceless metals. It was double-bladed and boxy, runes etched into the edges and borders. Even though it was simply magic and not the real thing, Astrid found herself drifting closer, pulled in through sight alone.

"Mjolnir," Tyr stated. "The unbeatable hammer."

Astrid glanced toward Thor. He had a newfound air about him. The trouble with the Jotunn had made him defeated and angry. Suddenly, with the image of the hammer slowly fading away, a fire was lit within the prince's stormy eyes. Astrid wondered what would've happened if she stepped forward, told Tyr to find another group of gods to fetch another artifact for the Aesir.

Lord Tyr's purple eyes snapped over to her, his expression ending her thoughts instantly.

"Tell the All-Father to consider it done, Lord Tyr," Thor stated.

"Very well, my Prince."

The ashy tree began to close and creak before anyone else could manage out another word. Loki's grip over Sigyn's hip grew exponentially tighter.

"What makes you so certain, *Prince Thor,* that we might be able to uncover a hammer in the land of Dwarves?" Loki spat, his voice crawling around like a snake.

Thor shook his head as he turned around slowly, hands on his hips. Blonde hair fell around his face, spilling out from the short tail behind his head. "Ridiculous," he murmured. "Are you telling me that my party is unable to think of any way for us to find the weapon? Not even one of you?"

"Great to see you still pull your weight, Thor," Sigyn muttered with an eye roll.

Thor ignored her as he snapped his fingers in Ullr's direction. "You've been around, Ullr. I'm sure you have a contact or two."

Ullr frowned as he thought and shrugged. "I might know a Dwarf."

"One who can get us into the labyrinth?" Loki raised a brow.

"Sure," Ullr replied. "He's a Dwarf, isn't he? They all know about the mines and the mazes." He gestured at the tree. "Open another portal, Sigyn. I will lead the way forward."

Loki shook his head. "Thor," he whispered, the venom gone from his voice. "Take heed in my words. We are out of our bounds. Svartalfheim is—"

"How many times do you need to stand in my way today, trickster?" Thor turned to face him, his unsteady anger slowly crossing his eyes another time. It wasn't as crazed as before, but rather intentful, determined, willing to do something the rest of them might regret later. He tilted his head ever so slightly, testing. "There is no piece of the Nine Realms that is out of my bounds. I thought you would understand that by now."

Sigyn finished pulling the portal out of the center of the tree, urging the bark apart till it split and cracked. Thor threw his pack over his shoulder, motioning for Ullr to step through first. The archer guard disappeared within the misty reflection, the colors changing shape as the destination took hold. Thor marched through next, his confidence unavoidable.

Loki glanced around. "Good luck to us all," he whispered before slipping into the portal.

Gripping the strap of her quiver, Astrid held her breath as she walked toward the tree. She never quite got used to portals. It was not like stepping through an open door or falling into the ocean waves. The feeling resembled going to sleep, not knowing where the dream would open, whether or not it would be a nightmare. Astrid hated every bit of it. The gods never had that sensation, she knew.

An icy cold grip snatched onto her wrist.

Astrid jerked around. "Sigyn," she said, fear spiking in her chest for a split, stupid second.

"I wish I could see whatever it is Loki sees in you," whispered Sigyn. Her voice was still and quiet. Unsettling.

Astrid held her mouth shut.

"But I am burdened with the truth," she continued, her eyes wide and echoing like the night sky. "You are just like him, aren't you?"

"Like who?"

"Your coyness was once admirable." Sigyn shook her head, releasing her tight grip on Astrid's arm. "Now, it is humiliating." She nodded at the portal. "He will be the death of you. Can't you see that?

Astrid looked forward. The reflection burnt a deep red and maroon, a flare of orange spiking through it every now and then, like a pulse. It was hard not to grow entranced, to not fall through it like a drunk, without any control. The sorceress's words echoed through the back of her mind as she stared, the haunting feeling she always had lingering effortlessly rising to the surface.

It was the feeling of death, mortality.

"Yes," she replied.

And Astrid stepped through the portal and into the land of Dwarves.

SIX

"Welcome to Storby, my friends."

Svartalfheim remained an elusive creation within the Nine Realms. Mazes and labyrinths made up most of it, with gaps between the winding halls that gave way for bustling towns. Storby was one of the largest settlements before the expansive labyrinth that happened to be run by the Dwarf, Ivaldi. It held everything a miner would've needed before heading to work and, possibly, an unavoidable death. There was a tavern, of course, a few brothels scattered about, a healer's tent too small to be noticed, and a government hall that gathered an innumerable amount of dust.

The portal opened behind a pawn shop, where the sounds of Dwarves lining up out the door with jingling bags of gold echoed like a faraway murmur. The unlucky miners who came across things not valuable enough went to the pawn shop, it seemed, to walk away with some fortune.

Ullr reached into the satchel at his belt, retrieving a small nub of ash. "No need for all those layers," he said, gesturing toward the company's large coats and gloves. "Off with it, my loves."

"We should remain inconspicuous, Ullr," Astrid said, holding onto her brown cloak tightly. Not only that, but it was the luckiest thing she owned, the last hood her father wore. There were a few things she carried on her person that kept her bound to her forgotten home: her father's worn and tattered cloak, a rock her mother carved a protection rune upon, and half of a dirty blonde braid, the hair wispy and coarse where it had been sliced. They were mementos she kept close to her heart, things she was unwilling to show to the gods, to the beings who did not understand what it meant to cherish a shortened life.

Ullr wiggled the ash in the air. "That's what the rune sorcery's for, spitfire."

Behind her, the cloak was gently tugged away by Thor. He stepped forward, already dressed simply, without a lick of armor. He tossed the cloaks into a pile on the ground beside the pawn shop. Astrid watched with wide eyes, her heart aching for a moment longer than she wanted it to. Though she could not possibly know for sure, her own voice echoed in the back of her mind: *I do not think I will see it again.* They would not go back for it, she knew. The gods she traveled with would not know the difference.

How could they?

It was just a cloak.

Thor lazily draped an arm over her shoulders. "What's next, Ullr?"

He twirled the ash around before striking it against his porcelain-colored skin. A kaleidoscope of color burst against the ground as he dragged the nub of ash along himself, despite there being no light above. A few lines struck against his forearm before twisting around his elbow. They burned bright for a moment, sinking deep into the god's statuesque skin, before simmering out into a simply done drawing.

"And to think," Loki mused from behind them, "I trained you to do...absolutely nothing."

Ullr stuck his tongue out. "I thought you'd be proud! Made the rune myself. I call it 'ansiktsløs[1].'"

"Well, that's fine and all, but what the hell does it do?"

"All of you of little faith," Ullr mumbled. "Though *we* recognize each other, the rune renders us disguised. Of course, the magic won't last very long, but—"

"Brilliant!" Thor pulled himself off Astrid, already extending his arm. "Me next."

Astrid stepped back as the gods moved forward, allowing Ullr to draw the rune over their bare arms. When they were all said and done, she rolled up her thin sleeve, about to extend herself over to the archer god. He twirled the ash in his fingers before dropping it back in his pocket, giving her a sideways frown.

"Sorry, love," he cooed. "You don't need ansiktsløs."

"Why not?" The offense she took to being excluded stung more than she wanted it to. Another reason that divided her from the only people she knew.

Thor reached for her next, as if he felt her sadness and grew so pitiful that he couldn't ignore her. He tucked a finger beneath her

---

1. Translation: Faceless.

chin, holding her angular face up toward him. Without thinking, she tried to pull away, but his grip was unwavering. Shame threatened to crawl up her throat, and despite craving to hide it, Thor noticed in seconds. And, like he always did, he wished to look at her shame, as if it was something to gawk at, something to study.

Even though Astrid was tall compared to the average Asgardian, Thor loomed over her, standing a few heads taller, like the rest of the gods.

"There isn't a soul in Svartalfheim who'd recognize you." Thor pinched her chin. "Wouldn't want to hide that face, now would we?"

Astrid's brow furrowed, using frustration to mask the pleasure that was trying to swarm up her throat. *Do not let him see. Do not let him know that he is both your lover and executioner.*

The god laughed to himself before releasing his hold on her and peering around the corner of the pawn shop. "Where would you have us headed, Ullr?"

"Well, the only way into the labyrinth is with a Dwarf as a guide." Ullr twisted through the company, stepping into the dim and amber firelight that illuminated the mining town. "And I happen to know one who is rather...how should I put it? *Empathetic* to the gods."

Loki rolled his eyes. "Is that supposed to convince us?"

"C'mon." Ullr nodded over his shoulder and curved around the stone building. The rest of the company followed close behind.

The city of Storby barely saw an outsider visit the realm. The labyrinths were impossible to navigate without a Dwarf. The gold and riches that lay deep within belonged to them, a part of their ancestry, and it was rare for others to venture within the mazes for treasure. Even with their disguises, the Dwarves eyed them warily as they walked by. Their gazes clung to Astrid as she gripped onto the strap of her quiver, a panic festering in the back of her mind that ached for violence, for the twitch of the bowstring.

Ullr effortlessly led them through Storby. Walls as tall as the mountains that bordered Asgard circled the city, deeply red streaks of Svartalfheim's core pulsating and beating through it. There were rowdy groups of brawling Dwarves, loitering on the corners and stumbling out of taverns, full mugs still in hand. Some sharpened their blades outside the blacksmith's door, others ripping the posters once left by Aesir soldiers off their stone walls.

Astrid's attention was caught. She reached, instinctively tugging on the end of Loki's cloak.

He didn't even stumble. "Yes, farmer girl?"

"Those posters," she whispered. "Is it—"

"Propaganda?" Loki smirked, his gaze landing on the vandalized art done of Odin, a phrase scrawled beneath his portrait.

The One-Eyed Fool.

Loki sighed. "The Aesir have had their foot within Svartalfheim for quite some time. I'm surprised you didn't know."

"How would I?"

"Oh," he drawled, "you mean the loyal Royal Guard doesn't know every little movement her beloved gods make?" He waggled a finger at her, shaking his head in a teasing manner. "Naughty, naughty, little farmer girl. The gods would be disappointed."

She narrowed her eyes at him. "Says the god."

Ullr held a tavern door open with his foot, gesturing boister-ously for the rest to follow. The sign above the door swung despite the lack of a breeze. Pale green stonework had a piggish snout carved upon it, a fluted horn erected from its mouth. Words were painted around the image: *The Boar's Horn.*

All of them slipped within the dark tavern, except Thor, who lingered at the threshold as Astrid approached. She gripped onto the strap of her quiver, ignoring how his presence brought an unbearable heat beneath her skin. Before she could slip inside, Thor snatched her bicep, his fingers latching entirely around her limb. He gripped tightly, possessively.

Astrid looked up at him, the breath catching in the back of her throat for a stupid, weak second. "Why're you looking at me like that?" she whispered.

"Like what?"

She pressed her lips together. For once, she would not give him the satisfaction of a response. The answers ran amok in her head: *like you might rip me in half, like you might sew me back together.*

Thor leaned closer, a wicked smile tugging his lip up. "You are mine," he hissed. "*Only* mine." His gaze snapped into the inside of the tavern, his attention falling upon Loki. "Do not forget that."

He released her quickly and walked into The Boar's Horn as if he hadn't said a single word.

Astrid swallowed down the growing lump in her throat and followed. She hated the desire that rested within her, the desire to let him take her, to let him be wild, to let him treat her like a possession he shaped with his own hands. But she loved him like a dog, a creature with sharp canines and a hunger for blood. Like a monster. Astrid would let him, she knew. She always knew.

The tavern was filled to the brim. A stage was erected on the eastern side, directly across from the curved, wooden bar. Dwarves with beards as long as their legs loitered in every corner, drowning themselves in sweet-smelling mead. Signs pinned to the walls called for more miners, more loot, more diamonds, and precious metals. Some boasted about Ivaldi and his labyrinth, others once held the image of the All-Father, only to be shredded or painted over maliciously.

Astrid's eyes clung to the imagery. Painted posters pinned to the walls with thick nails held images of the King of Asgard, seated upon the Bleeding Throne. What was meant to be a symbol of great power, of justice, had starkly red lines dragged across it, calling the king names Astrid never wished to repeat.

False god. Evil king. Executioner.

The world around her moved in slow motion. The last word, *executioner*, echoed across her vision. No longer did she watch where she walked or even bothered to notice the brawl beginning to grow rowdy at the front of the bar. The company left her behind, moving towards the stage and watching the fight with obvious amusement.

But she could not look away. Something sparked in her chest.

My king, scorned.

My king...their villain?

My king—

The side of Astrid's face collided with sturdy, iron armor, reeking of dirt and musk. She stumbled backwards, knocking into a few drinkers.

"*Oi!*" the Dwarf in front of her exclaimed. His mug clattered to the floor, staining the leather shoes he wore. Shimmering blue eyes were hidden behind a bushy brow, an even longer beard to match. He stood a foot shorter than Astrid, but raised his fist all the same, already launching a punch toward her.

Thor appeared at her side like a bolt of lightning. His hand snapped out, grabbing the Dwarf's fist in midair. "Touch her," the prince murmured in an eerily calm voice, eyes blazing with a thunderous anger, "and I'll *fucking* break your neck."

Blessed be the Raven God, for he has delivered unto me an unchained beast.

Astrid watched the prince with an unwavering stare. To all things holy, Astrid prayed to have a good enough reason to abandon her deadly devotion to Thor. But, in moments like those, the bond that tied them together shuddered and tightened.

And who was she to break such a beautiful thing?

The Dwarf gulped loudly as the god released his hold over him.

Astrid allowed Thor to tug her against him, to guide her toward the rest of their company. Eyes held onto her, the judgment and disgust sinking into her skin. Though she was never one to truly care, it was the darkness in Loki's stare that threatened to render her into nothing but stone.

Ullr managed to wrangle a secluded table within the tavern, sitting partly in shadow. A crowd loomed over the stage, where a rather nimble-looking Dwarf tried to perform badly written poetry. Astrid took her seat between Loki and Thor, the tension heavy in the back of her throat. Loki leaned away, putting deliberate space between them.

So childish, she thought. Instantly, she felt like a piece of dog-shit.

Ullr nodded toward the stage. "The lucky man."

"You're..." Sigyn's stare narrowed. "You're joking."

"Not at all."

The performing Dwarf carried his unnaturally light-colored hair in a plume, a tall curl erecting from the top. Not a single hair stepped out of place, none upon his chin or above his lip. Everything remained neatly clipped and trimmed. But perhaps it wasn't even that that was the most peculiar thing about him.

Dwarves spent their time underground, rendering their hair coarse and dark, capable of stopping the minerals and dirt from scoring their skin. And the complexion they held was paler than the moon itself. Not a glimmer of sunlight ever touched them. Even so, the Dwarf upon the stage was as magnetic as amber, freshly harvested from the base of an elderly tree. Astrid was stunted by the Dwarf's unusual beauty, unsure of entirely what she was looking at in the first place.

"To swallow thine mind, to refrain that pain," the Dwarf proclaimed in a musical voice. "Heidrun, Heidrun, come sleep beside me once a'gain!"

The tavern burst into an uproar of laughter and shouts of displeasure. Full mugs of ale flew before splattering at the Dwarf's feet. He stuttered and flinched, the purple curls of his waistcoat and suit stained and ruined.

"Did he just..." Astrid blinked a few times and shook her head. "Did he just say he sleeps with Heidrun? The goat?"

"Isn't he wonderful?" Ullr clapped and cheered, earning a few disgruntled looks from the other audience members.

"A flyting Dwarf," Loki murmured, his eyes wide. "Perhaps now I *have* seen it all."

Astrid tilted her head. "I wouldn't call that flyting," she said. "There is hardly a rhyme about it."

A burly laugh came from the other side of her, Thor's presence like an enveloping sun against her mortal skin. He leaned over the table, a wicked and handsome smile tugging at his lip. "We ought to take the thing home with us," he teased. "Have a great performance for the Aesir!"

The laughter carried around the table, but Astrid could hardly join in. She watched the audience berate the Dwarf, forcing him to stumble off the stage and awkwardly stagger away. He didn't even have the opportunity to slip into the crowd, to blend in with the rest of his people. The boy still stood out like a sore thumb.

Astrid softened like a fool.

Ullr waved the Dwarf over before he could sulk in the corner. "Absolutely *wonderful* performance, my friend!" He rose from his seat to shake the Dwarf's nimble hand. "Take a seat, won't you? I've already got a mug o' mead." The wooden mug spilled foam over the side as he pushed it across the table.

"Oh," the Dwarf mouthed. "How...kind. But alas"—he pushed the mug back with a narrow finger— "I do not drink."

"What sort of Dwarf doesn't drink?" Thor fell back against his seat and shook his head slowly. "Ullr, tell me where you found this peculiar little creature."

"I'd prefer to be called something *other* than 'peculiar little creature,'" the Dwarf mumbled. "Though, you lot look as though you could pummel me without lifting a finger."

Astrid sighed. Gods weren't the most appropriately social type. "Tell us your name, poet."

"Oh," he said again, cheeks turning a delicate shade of pink. "Poet would do."

"Your *name*," Astrid laughed.

He gulped again, straightening up instantly. "Solaris Carnelius the Third." He bowed his head boisterously. "At your service."

Astrid blinked a few times. "You're...what?"

Around the table, the gods grew silent, all of them eyeing the Dwarf with a raised brow.

He shrank down into a hunched position, avoiding their stares. "The name is Darrow," he mumbled. "As in, son of Marrow."

"Why the fake name?"

"What you might call a *fake name*, my lady," Darrow began, his voice rising with every word. He slowly stood up, arms gesturing greatly to either side of him, fingers just barely grazing the top of a nearby Dwarf's head. "Is more like a *stage name,* as I am the one and only famed bard in all of Svartalfheim!"

Jeering grew loud all around them for a second time, a half-eaten loaf of bread and a holey mound of cheese slapping the side of Darrow's face. He collapsed against the chair, defeated. The final sound of his tune was his forehead smacking the wooden table.

"Well," Darrow weakly uttered, "at least I will always be the one and only bard in all of Svartalfheim."

Astrid's patience grew thin. "Ullr," she snapped, trying to keep her voice low, "how in the Nine Realms is *he* supposed to be our guide through the labyrinth?"

Darrow's widening eyes grabbed onto Astrid. His loud gulp filled the gap in conversation as he slowly glanced behind him. A few nearby Dwarves, deep in their mugs of mead, watched the company over their shoulders. When Darrow turned back to her, he leaned forward and pulled at his shimmering collar, sweat pooling around the thick fabrics.

Fear, Astrid realized. It followed the labyrinth around like a shadow.

"Y-You're...you're going to the labyrinth?" he asked in a low whisper.

The company eyed Darrow instantly, clocking his sudden interest.

"Yes," Thor answered, his teasing slipping out the door. "What of it?"

Darrow twitched and fidgeted around in his squeaking chair. His voice came out in a trembling mumble. "My father was one of the original builders of Ivaldi's mine. The blueprints"—he tapped his temple— "lie within me."

Ullr sighed, lazily draping his hands on the back of his neck. "Every last one of you," he murmured with a smirk, "creatures of little faith."

Astrid shook her head. "How can you be a bard?"

"Does being a Dwarf make me a miner?" Darrow shrugged. "I do not believe it does. The gift of writing, of rhyming. I was born with it, not a connection to the mines."

"That doesn't help us," Astrid murmured. "We require a guide through Ivaldi's labyrinth. One that might assist us in retrieving something very valuable."

Darrow's thin brow rose. "What," he sputtered. "You mean the hammer?"

"How can you—"

"Everyone in Svartalfheim knows about Mjolnir," Darrow said. "It made Ivaldi famous. He runs the show around here because of it." He pressed his lips together and pulled away, suspicion filling his almond-shaped eyes. "What makes you think Ivaldi would allow some..." His frown deepened. "Aesir into his labyrinth?"

Ullr waved at him dismissively. "*Allow* wouldn't be the word we're concerned with, my friend. Get us inside, and we'll handle the rest."

"Well, you make it sound so simple. You'd have to get through the labyrinth itself first," he explained. "One that never remains the same, that has a will of its own. If you manage to survive it, Mjolnir sits at the very center, guarded for all eternity by the strongest pair of Dwarves in all of Svartalfheim. Brokkr and Sindri. They"—he paused to huff a few times—"Are *nothing* to scoff at."

Astrid knew the resilience of her company without even needing to look at them. Perhaps the path before them was far too risky, a death wish waiting to happen. Dwarves were terrifyingly strong creatures and managed to craft weapons capable of killing a god. Fear should have been at the forefront of their hearts.

A smirk crawled across Astrid's face.

What is fear?

"Can you lead us or not?"

Darrow glanced around. "J-Just like that?"

"We need a guide," Astrid said. "A Dwarven one, to be exact. Perhaps you aren't a good Dwarf, but you are one, all the same."

Darrow blinked a few times, the hesitation evident in the way his fingers rattled against the table. "I..." His voice trailed off as he pressed his lips together. When he looked up again, there was a newfound and unmistakable determination. "I will lead you through Ivaldi's labyrinth," he stated. "*If* you all agree to let me journey alongside you and record your adventure so that I might be the famed bard of Svartalfheim."

The company remained silent, instinctively awaiting their leader to decide.

Thor watched the Dwarf with narrow eyes, his expression unreadable. He stared closely, not a single word leaving his lips.

"Prince," Loki whispered. "Perhaps we might—"

"Consider it done, Darrow son of Marrow." Thor extended his hand across the table. "A great company deserves an even greater bard, doesn't it?"

Darrow's face lit up as he shook Thor's hand, the plume of hair at the top of his head bouncing. "You won't be sorry!"

Maybe it was the hope on the Dwarf's face, or the displeasure upon Loki's that made Astrid grow incredibly haunted within The Boar's Horn. The adventure that awaited them did not feel worthy of a bard's song, to be praised for as long as Yggdrasil's roots strung the realms together.

No, she thought. *It does not.*

SEVEN

Ivaldi's private mansion sat atop a short hill within Storby.

A backdrop of tall mountainous walls streaked with burning red heat was behind the tall house. Iron gates stood like sharp pillars upon each corner of the mansion, the Dwarvish language garish and starkly written upon the front entrance. Guards dressed in blinding silver patrolled each side, wading around the gates slowly and purposefully. Above, where there was no sky, but rather a never-ending stretch of a wooden-like surface, Astrid slid down a tightrope, her bow curved around the wire.

Wind funneled around her as she sped further and further down, aiming for the mansion's rooftop. A pair of Dwarven guards loitered along the edge, their backs facing her. They looked over Storby with a peculiarly perfect view. Ivaldi's mansion managed to overlook the entire town before the labyrinth, from one end, all the way to the other.

The bow trembled in her grasp as she slid, but never once faltered.

Praise the Asketre, she thought to herself. *A cursed wood, but practically unbreakable.*

The guards wore thick silver armor that shone so bright it stung Astrid's eyes as she propelled closer to them.

"The Sølv they wear is the strongest known armor in all the Nine Realms," Darrow had warned earlier that day. "End them quietly and firmly, or you won't stand a chance."

Astrid never considered herself to be too brave for her own good, but as the Dwarf spoke to her, all she did was hold back her smirk. They had convened in a darkened alleyway before venturing out to Ivaldi's private estate, forming a plan as quickly as they could. "Simple," she replied. "All armor has its weakness." She nodded her chin towards the others. "What will they do?"

Loki had one arm tightly curled around Sigyn's waist. "We will clear the way from the ground while you show off in the skies."

"Really?" Astrid's brow rose. "You'll let me go on my own?"

Sigyn's lip curled. "Is that fear I hear?"

"More like excitement." Astrid had twirled her bow in front of her. "I'll get it done."

Darrow was scribbling in a small book when he spoke again. "Ullr will travel to my family home," he explained. "We will collect a key for the labyrinth from my father."

"Oh," Astrid had drawled. "The famous Marrow?"

The Dwarf frowned and pulled at his collar as his face took on a sickly grey shade. "Don't remind me."

The plan unfolded rather quickly, and the next thing Astrid knew, she was barreling down to the mansion's rooftop all on her lonesome. Somewhere within Storby, Thor remained in the streets, collecting 'intel', as he liked to call it.

The rooftop came rushing forward as the wire began to come to an end. The hook she shot from yards away dug deep into the stone, the tip shaking as gravity pulled her down. Astrid extended her feet, holding her breath, and hit the ground running. The pads of her feet were silent against the ground as she ran forward, slipping the bow in her quiver and retrieving a sleek sword the same length as her forearm. It wasn't anything brilliant or overdramatic, but a carving blade, one to use when faced with a dead animal. The gods thought her to be small and weak with only a short blade to protect her.

But what they didn't understand was simple.

The weak were merely frightened; her fear bred violence.

Astrid's thin sword struck the first guard in the back of the knees, where the Sølv did not cover. A grunt filled the air, surprising them first before they had a chance to turn around. She pulled the blade, hearing the muscles tear and shudder against her strike. Astrid straightened, puncturing the second guard through the neck.

Ignore the blood.

The first reached for the hilt of his axe upon his belt. Her sword slipped through the second and sliced through the air before returning to the first, capturing the nape of his throat maliciously.

Ignore the blood.

Astrid jerked the sword out, and the body crumbled, a splatter of inky red blood splashing across the dark leather armor she wore.

How do I ignore what I am?

One of the Dwarven guards twitched on the ground, his chest heaving as life slowly trickled away from him. Dark and desperate eyes held onto her. "A-Are...you...*death*?"

The breath caught in her throat. "No," she finally managed, but it was a lie. "Sometimes."

He was dead before he could hear her reply.

Footsteps came from behind her, slow and casual.

"Thor's shadow," Loki mused. "I see why they call you that."

Astrid dragged the long blade across her arm, the blood leaving a dripping trail against the leather sleeve. Her eyes clung to it despite the guilt beginning to burrow its way through the center of her chest. "I do not," she murmured.

Sigyn curled around Loki, her similar armor beautifully clinging to her skin. She was a creature of deadly power, and yet, looked like a piece of the fallen night sky. Her long braids were tied together at the top of her head, held out of her face with a bright silver band. She eyed Astrid with a raised, slender brow.

"Perhaps you should take their armor, farmer girl," Sigyn teased. "You might need it."

Astrid glanced down at the dead Dwarves. "Doesn't look all that great to me."

"We ought to hurry in," Loki murmured as he loomed over the edge of the rooftop. "Besides, our little farmer girl doesn't need any armor. She has shown us that before, hasn't she?"

"I do not know how many times I need to tell you *not* to call me that."

"Oh," he drawled, growing more amused by the second. "My sincerest apologies. Did you prefer Thor's Shadow?"

Astrid rolled her eyes and slid her blade through her belt. "The trap door is this way."

Darrow told the company that any information regarding Ivaldi's upcoming plans would be stored away in his private mansion. It was built only recently, when Ivaldi managed to rise to power within Storby in the past few months. According to the bard, Ivaldi hosted numerous outsiders within his halls, though they weren't entirely sure who. Astrid was more concerned with slipping in and out without being caught, all the while trying to find the map that would lead the way through the labyrinth.

The trap door was near the center of the rooftop. One of the Dwarven guards carried a silver key that unlocked it within a second, causing the wooden door to fall open with ease. Loki waved over the entrance.

"After you, my dear ladies."

Sigyn let her gloved hand slide across his face before she slipped inside, disappearing within the darkness. Astrid peered through the trap door and saw shadows dance across her vision.

"Are you afraid?"

She met Loki's deeply dark stare. "Why would I be?"

"I don't see your knight around," Loki murmured, leaning against his arm lazily as he held open the trap door. "Does that make you afraid?"

"Of you?"

Loki shrugged, nonchalant and casual, but Astrid saw the question dancing in his eyes.

"No."

"Liar."

"I am not afraid," Astrid snapped, one leg falling through the trap door. She grew tired of the tricksters' teasing. His motive remained unseen, but it was there. "We have a job to do, remember?"

"Oh, I remember."

"I'm not sure you do."

Dimples protruded from Loki's cheeks as his grin grew. He was far too amused. "Has anyone ever told you the fable of the bear and the deer?"

Astrid groaned like a child. "For the first time in all my life," she whispered, "I'd much rather be dealing with your wife right now."

Down below, already within Ivaldi's mansion, Sigyn released a loud snort.

Loki twirled a finger in the air, flashing magenta colored nails at her. Purple mist seeped out of his palm and swirled around him like a slow hanging fog, curling around his braided locks, tucking beneath his robes as though his magic was an old friend.

"Once, there was a bear," Loki retold in a musical voice. "It was a harrowing beast that searched for the deer every day of its life. Here and there it went—" The mist took shape, resembling a grizzly Astrid might've encountered in the woods surrounding her family farm.

The purple, misty creature galloped across the thin air before reaching her shoulder and running around her neck. It came to her opposite side, and Astrid raised her arm, letting the grizzly bear run along the length of it. When the beast leapt off her index finger, a laugh escaped her lips, and her mouth snapped shut. She hadn't realized there was even a smile on her face.

Astrid's eyes snapped towards Loki, and his stare was heavy with a shadowy darkness.

"Always searching, always hungry."

Astrid frowned, hating how intrigued she'd become during his stories. "Loki."

"*But...*" Loki's fingers danced in the air, swiping and sliding, the mist forming a series of runes. Out from between the sharp lines, a slender deer burst through, galloping delicately across the air. It bounced over Astrid's gaze, landing upon her shoulder before curling back toward Loki. "When the bear finally came across its prized deer, there was something *more* than happiness there. Something *hungry*."

The grizzly bear stepped over Loki's shoulder, hunching down at the sight of its prey. Loki's fingers twitched, and the beast clobbered down before letting its paws collapse around the deer's narrow neck. The touch, though deadly and violent, reminded Astrid of a sort of peculiar tenderness. A need to keep the sacred clean, innocent, despite being unable to fight the urge to tear it apart yourself.

"I suppose you might be able to tell what happened next."

Sharp teeth sank into the deer's throat. There was an exhale, a whispering gasp. The bear collected each drop of blood, licking the dying deer's unstoppable wounds. The tenderness behind the beast was almost heartwarming. No matter how uncomfortable Astrid became, she could not pull her eyes away.

Loki dragged his hand through the apparition. The expression he wore was testing, intent. "Tell me, farmer girl," he whispered. "Did the bear love the deer?"

"No," she blurted.

Liar.

Astrid kept the truth behind her clenched teeth. Her instinctive answer, the words that echoed in the back of her mind the moment he asked the question, rose to the very tip of her tongue.

Of course, the bear loved the dear. Isn't it obvious?

She thought of Thor. She thought of nights entangled within his silk sheets in the golden castle, the wide windows cast open to let the evening breeze tickle their bare skin. Her fingers slipped around the wispy blonde curls that danced across his chest. He would rise during the early morning to pick a ripe fruit from the vines that grew along the side of the castle. The sickly sweet red juice spilled across her chin like blood as he slipped the end between her teeth.

Astrid wanted to step out of her own body and sink into the floor.

"Lost in your thoughts, farmgirl?"

She scowled at him. "We are here for a reason, trickster."

Sliding both her legs through the trap door, Astrid fell through and entered Ivaldi's mansion.

"Oh."

Somehow, the door led directly into Ivaldi's office. The ornate room had pillars at every corner, silver and bronze melted into the very walls. Bookcases lined with ancient tomes decorated the walls, separated by glass cases that contained priceless artifacts. At the center of the room, directly in front of where Astrid landed, was a wide wooden desk with a leather chair behind it.

Sigyn lounged against the chair, her long and slender legs thrown across it lazily. There was a book in her hands, the pages frayed but lined with obvious molten gold. "Finally," she drawled as she snapped it shut. "How long did you two expect me to wait in here?"

"I was waiting for Astrid to remember why we are here, my beloved." Loki curled around Astrid as though he had been there before her, but that was impossible. Purple mist still followed him around closely. He stepped behind Sigyn and pressed a tender kiss to the top of her head.

"Silly girl," Sigyn murmured.

"What sort of idiot has a trap door directly above his private study?" Astrid muttered as she began to loom about the room. Far too much time was spent listening to Loki's incessant rambling, and they needed to hurry. There was no telling when Ivaldi would return home, or when another pair of guards would make their way to the rooftop.

A long glass case sat on the western side of the study, a few relics slumbering within. Astrid's curiosity drove her toward it, ignoring the plumes of papers and books she should've been paying attention to. Instead, she stared through the glass, fingers pressing greedily against it.

"A piece of Odin's Gungnir," she whispered. The ebony shard sat upon a short pedestal within the case. It glimmered despite a lack of light, pulsating as if it carried a heart beneath the stone. The power radiated through the case, though dulled slightly. Astrid felt it against her fingertips, almost tempting her to break the glass with a fist. "Ivaldi *is* a master blacksmith, isn't he? If he built such a thing as the All-Father's unbeatable weapon."

"Everything is beatable," Loki said from behind her as he leaned against the desk.

She shook her head. "How can something forged from blessed Ymir's blood be beatable?"

"You tell me, farmer girl."

But Astrid wasn't paying attention to her companions any longer. Their casual nature was beginning to drive her mad, and the last thing she needed was an untoward outburst.

Beside the shard taken from Gungnir was a replica of Mjolnir, a stunning boxed hammer with a handle studded with complex runes. Astrid stepped over to it, her fingers following the runes on the glass. Despite it only being a model used to craft the real thing, something tugged her forward, tempting her toward it once again. Astrid bit down upon her lip till inky iron dripped between her teeth.

Astrid pulled away from the glass and looked over her shoulder toward the lazy pair. They merely draped themselves over the desk, their gazes flickering about without a sense of urgency. Looking back at the glass, her gloved hands tightened against the case. "Do either one of you even care about this mission?"

Loki chuckled. "If we cared for every mission the All-Father sent us on, we'd hardly ever return to Asgard, now would we?"

"This weapon is capable of incredible destruction," she murmured as she stared into the hammer. "To not bring it home would be the same as placing it in the hands of our greatest foe."

"Don't be so dramatic." Sigyn twirled around in her seat.

Dramatic? Astrid simmered like a fuse. "Why don't both of you keep an eye out on the roof? I might find the map without distraction."

Sigyn sighed heavily. "You are not who I answer to, farmer girl. Besides, do you honestly think you can handle this yourself? What if Ivaldi comes home? What if more of his guards happen to trickle inside? What then?"

"I do not need you."

Loki chuckled. "Relax, Astrid."

"Relax?" She snapped as she whipped around. "How might I relax when we are tasked with uncovering a map that neither one of you seems bothered enough to find?"

"We are here with you, aren't we?"

Astrid flipped back to the case, glancing toward a cabinet that contained a series of ledgers and journals. "If I were by myself—"

Sigyn's sharp and short laugh filled the study. "Don't tell me the little farmer girl believes she might be better off without her gods."

Astrid's stubbornness filled her throat like bile. "Look at you both," she hissed, waving a hand over their casually laid-back natures. "Acting as if we are simply taking a stroll through a Dwarf's house." She shook her head. "You *gods*."

"Go on." Sigyn straightened and glared, a silvery power beginning to course through her eyes. "Keep going, farmer girl. Keep digging your own grave."

Tight fists rested at Astrid's side as she avoided looking at the sorceress. There was only so much she could handle, so much teasing, so much mocking, before the ticking bomb within her was incapable of simmering out. When Astrid faced them again, she hardly recognized herself as human any longer, only feeling the rays of golden divinity that pulsed off her companions.

"Leave," she growled, "And I will find the map *myself*."

Loki leaned forward, his brow furrowed tightly, but before he could speak, his wife extended her hand, gloved fingertips brushing the center of his chest gently. He eyed her but backed down without uttering a single word.

"Do you think you can be rid of us so easily?"

Astrid bit back a bitter laugh. "It's as simple as—"

"But you have tasted it."

She blinked. "I-I don't—"

"The sweetness, the bitterness." Sigyn leaned back into Ivaldi's wide chair, twisting around in a half circle, but her eyes—those sharp, unavoidable eyes—never *once* left her. "You drank it in like a child's first taste of wine: eagerly, foolishly, dependently.

You'll reach for it, again and again, with those *greedy* little mortal fingers." She smirked. "You think we don't know?"

"What the hell are you talking about?" *Do not tell me. I do not want to know.*

But Sigyn was already looming, already knowing she'd say the words. "The divinity," she murmured. "It's addicting, isn't it?"

Astrid was rendered frozen in place, hands still pressed against the glass case. Their presence suffocated her, suddenly, rather than giving her more life. But, most of all, it was how they watched, how they never let their eyes pull away, that burrowed the blade of shame further into her chest.

When she spoke, there was barely a whisper. "I'm not—"

"Isn't it interesting how it rubs off on you?" Sigyn wondered, holding one hand up to her eyes, as if she could see golden blood coursing underneath her skin. "The immortal soul leaves its footprint against your skin. It'll fade, of course, but that's just what pulls you back in." Her hand slammed down upon the desk, pulling a sharp flinch out of Astrid. "Get off your high horse. You need us just as much as we need you, and even if you didn't, you're far too addicted to our divinity now to leave it all behind."

Astrid watched them over her shoulder, stunned into speechlessness. It was as if the sorceress peeled her skin back to leave a simple casing, one that was empty and hollow. There was a minuscule creature living within her, what one might call the *soul*, and it had beckoning hands, desperate to be touched and held by the gods she put upon an unreachable pedestal.

Sigyn, seemingly satisfied, leaned back casually in her chair, raising her shoulders in a shrug. When she lifted her hand, there was a thick piece of papyrus held up between her fingers. The hearty Dwarvish language was scored across it, only two of the words recognizable to Astrid, who lacked a good understanding of Svartalfheim's language.

Map and *Labyrinth.*

"So, I'll ask again," Sigyn murmured as she held up the prize Astrid had been stupidly searching for. "Did you think you could be rid of us so easily?"

Embarrassment snatched onto her throat so easily, eager to spill out between her lips and fall across Ivaldi's study floor. She marched toward the desk, bending at the waist to reach over and snatch the paper out from Sigyn's grasp.

The sorceress jerked the page away, dangling in the air. "Not so fast, farmer girl," she whispered. "We can't risk you misplacing our prize, now, can we?"

Astrid's hand foolishly slammed against the top of the desk. She hardly cared anymore if there were patrolling guards or if even Ivaldi was making his way back to his mansion. All she could think about was how much of an idiot she felt like, how much of a mortal she was between the two gods. Her eyes fell, staring at the green-blue veins that coursed beneath her skin.

Mortality, she thought, *haunts me still.*

Papers squished and flattened beneath her fingers caught Astrid's attention. Finally, there wasn't an unrecognizable or un-readable Dwarvish. She tilted her head, eyes rapidly scanning the text before one of her companions thought it fun to tease or mock her some more.

Lord Blacksmith and Governor of Storby, the Vanir graciously accept your invitation into your realm, and very much look forward to a personal tour of your famed labyrinths. Our Council is—

"Hold on," Astrid murmured, twisting the page around to get a better look at the handwriting. "This is...this is..."

Our Council is honored to take your new creation off your burdened hands.

"Did you two see this?" Astrid held the letter up. "Doesn't this mean that—"

For the first time since they entered the mansion, Loki's eyes grew wide, a haunting paleness spreading over his long and crooked nose. "*Faen alt sammen*[1]," he cursed and ripped the page out of her hands. "The Dwarves are selling Mjolnir to the Vanir."

Sigyn exhaled sharply. "Do the Aesir know?"

"I wondered why they sent us on this wild goose chase in the first place," he grumbled, the page almost ripping in his long fingers. "Damn it all, they must have known! And willingly put us face to face with the damned enemy!" Loki reached suddenly and snatched onto Astrid's arm. "Our beloved farmer girl. Where would we be if we didn't have you, hm?" His fingers squeezed her chin briefly before folding the letter up and sliding it within one of his pockets.

---

1. Translation: Fuck it all.

Grasping Sigyn's hand, Loki pulled her out from around the desk. "Come along, my loves," he cooed, nodding his chin toward the open trap door. "Up and out, as fast as you can."

"Loki," Astrid breathed, her heart hammering. "What does this mean?"

Sigyn was already halfway onto the roof, her legs dangling, before she managed to pull herself up the rest of the way.

The trickster hardly looked unbothered any longer. Fear—or perhaps it was something else, something she could not recognize—flashed across his aged face, all the time he spent living suddenly apparent on his skin.

"It means we are faced with something none of us are equipped to handle," he whispered.

"Do you mean to run?"

His brow furrowed. "I mean to *protect*," he hissed, grabbing her hand and forcibly pushing her toward the trap door.

Sigyn's long arms reached through and began to pull Astrid out of Ivaldi's mansion. An unusual breeze swept through her maroon hair, reeking of metal and iron and dirt. Loki appeared by their side instantly, snapping the trap door shut behind her.

Distant chatter grew closer as Dwarven guards began to make their way toward their next shift, nearing the rooftop with every step they took. Astrid scrambled to the opposite side, already grabbing her bow and another wire. Storby's city sat down the hill from Ivaldi's mansion, metallic buildings surrounded by shacks made from dirt too far for an arrow to hit. The wire wouldn't be able to get lodged anywhere for them to zip down it.

Astrid muttered a curse. "Unless you two have any bright ideas," she murmured, "we're going to be spotted."

The last thing they needed was to be recognized within the realm. The rune sorcery Ullr once drew upon the gods' skin barely lingered upon them any longer.

As the guards reached the ladder that would take them directly onto the roof, Loki's hands glowed a deep magenta, twirls of mist twirling around his long fingers. He stepped toward the ladder, the magic beginning to spread through the air when—

Oddly familiar shouts echoed out from Storby's center. The city was shaped like a rounded valley, with tall walls that marked the beginning of the mazes and labyrinths erected on all sides. Anything loud from within the city would surely reach them through echoes alone. But it was that sound, like yelling or whooping, that managed to bring an odd chill to Astrid's spine. Her eyes narrowed as it came again, and the Dwarven guards abandoned the ladder and ran toward the commotion.

Sigyn glanced around. "Tell me that isn't who I think it is."

But Loki was already running, already scaling down the side of the mansion without caring if a guard saw him. And as Sigyn followed, her words answered through his actions alone, Astrid felt stuck in place, an echoing shame beginning to surge toward the center of her chest.

It couldn't be...but it was.

"Thor."

EIGHT

"*F ight me!*"

Thunder boomed through Storby's rowdy courtyard. Dwarves flocked toward it to see the unbelievable spectacle, flinching and whooping as lightning struck the muddy ground. The sky was hardly visible in the Dwarven realm, but it was hardly necessary. Thor's power came from within—inherently, instinctively. As if there was a storm resting within his soul, ready to be brought forth whenever he saw fit.

The Boar's Horn's front doors were held open by onlooking Dwarves, their mugs of mead and ale dripping onto the ground as they watched the entertainment unfold. Thor stumbled through the street, shoving as many Dwarves as he wished. Blonde curls fell across his stormy eyes, his cheeks a bright red and drunken hue.

"*Someone!*" he slurred, whipping about like a madman. "Fight me!"

Astrid ran toward him. So many things rushed through her mind, all of them sounding off alarms within her. She needed to cover him, to protect him, to pull him into the shadows and silence all the eyes that wished to hold on. At the same time, anger bubbled up her throat, threatening to spill out in all the worst ways possible.

He is an idiot. A drunken, out-of-his-mind idiot.

She reached for her blade, moments away from slipping through the crowd of Dwarves.

"Wait!" Loki's hand tangled around her arm, yanking her around the side of a building. His black eyes glowed purple in the shadows. "Are you mad?"

"He needs to be protected!" Astrid hissed. "He needs to be—"

"Stopped," he interjected, his brow furrowed so tight a harsh wrinkle was beginning to appear on his forehead. "That's what you were going to say, right? He needs to be *stopped.*"

Behind him, Sigyn nodded, her stare just as heavy.

Astrid breathed heavily out of her nose, desperately trying to control the anger that simmered beneath her skin. She jerked her arm out of his grasp. "Grab me again, and see what happens, trickster."

"Oh, Thor's Shadow strikes again, doesn't she?"

"What do you suppose we do, then?" Astrid peered around the corner of the building. In the distance, coming from the same direction they did, Dwarven guards glimmering with heavy, silver armor approached in tight formation. She pulled herself back, glaring at Loki. "Well done, trickster. We waited, and now the guard's approach. You better have a plan."

"Once," Loki whispered, the tightness in his brow softening for a split second, "you believed in me, didn't you?"

The breath caught in the back of her throat. The shame, the disgust, he carried behind his eyes settled onto Astrid's chest and almost fell against the ground. She wanted to cower, to step out from within her skin and hide within the surrounding darkness. To have a friend look at her in such a way was more haunting than she realized.

Loki's fingers danced about as the purple mist spread through the air. "I'll provide cover," he murmured. "You and Sigyn will grab the baboon and run. We cannot stop running till we are hidden, till the guards cannot find us. Understood?"

Sigyn nodded, already slipping around the corner and blending into the shadows.

"You," Loki said, his voice firm.

Astrid looked up at him once more. "What, is there more you'd like to berate me with?"

He scowled, a frown tugging across his lips. "When will you see?"

"See what?"

"The drunken beast out there cares for little," Loki said, thrusting an angry finger toward the ruckus. "All he sees is red, and I am afraid you are nearing that inescapable fate alongside him. But you...you can still survive. You can survive *us*."

Astrid stared with her lips pressed together. Sigyn's words from Ivaldi's study came rushing back to her, echoing in the back of her mind like an unforgettable prayer.

You're far too addicted to our divinity now to leave it all behind.

"The cage you act like you are trapped in is wide open," he whispered. "Why can't you walk out?"

Her voice came out as a whisper. "You are wrong."

Loki shook his head like a disappointed father. "Fine," he replied. "Perhaps I am."

And before she could say another word, he slipped around the corner, purple smoke engulfing his legs.

Astrid gulped air as if she were about to be plunged underwater. She told herself that Darrow and Ullr were having better luck in an uncovering the key, and it calmed her down for a split second. Sheathing her short blade, she stepped out from the alleyway's cover, following in the sorceress's footsteps.

The Dwarves laughed and shouted in their garish language, pushing the drunken god when he came too close. Thor whipped his fists about wickedly, strings of lightning sparking around his fingertips. Astrid clung close to the walls, Sigyn's dark, cloaked figure practically invisible. Purple mist crawled between the Dwarves' legs, creeping closer and closer to the thunder god.

"*F-Fight—!*" Thor wailed as a mug of mead soared through the air and landed against his chest.

Loki's magic swallowed them whole in the same second.

The Dwarves went wild through Storby, hooting and hollering about a cursed magic filling their lungs. It was harmless, Astrid knew, but something about seeing them run around as if their worlds were ending struck a chord in her stomach. Thor flung his arms about like a lunatic, trying to claw his way through the mist.

Astrid sprinted out of the shadow and through the fog. Beside her, moving without making a sound, was the sorceress, disks of bright silver radiating around her hands.

"Thor," she snapped as she grabbed his wrists, feeling an erratic pulse beneath his skin. "*Thor,* look at me!"

Sharp eyes tainted with lines of red and exhaustion fell upon her. "My beloved," he slurred, one clammy hand wrapping around the back of her neck. "Come to fight me, haven't you?"

"You're drunk." Astrid jerked herself out of his loose hold, slipping one arm around his waist and gripping him tightly. He reeked of mead and ale, sour and pungent. "We need to go, before the mist clears!"

Sigyn led the way out of the fog, weaving in and around the group of frantic Dwarves.

"No!" Thor struggled against her, zaps of lightning scoring her mortal skin. "I must *fight,* I might—"

Loki materialized in front of them, a wild rage festering in his eyes. "You *must* run," he seethed. "Before I knock you out and take you forcibly, Prince."

Thor's face fell before a loud laugh rocked through them. "Trickster of Asgard," he slurred, one hand reaching for Loki's shoulder but only pressing against his sternum. "Come to save the day? Prove yourself?"

A darkness clouded the thunder god's expression as he fell heavily against Astrid's side. His arm snaked around her waist, fingers digging possessively through leather armor. "Come to take another woman from my arms?" Thor's lip curled, and he leaned closer to Astrid's temple, warm and heavy breath fanning over her cheek. "To claim my discarded sec—"

"*Forbannet tunge*[1] *!*" Loki hissed. He reached for Astrid, snatching her by the elbow and jerking her away from the prince. "Try to stand, Boulder, without having another innocent soul to lean upon!"

As if he had never been drunk in the first place, Thor straightened, lightning sparking between his eyes.

Astrid wished to be something as strong as the gods she worshiped, capable of moving mountains or calling a storm with nothing but her will. To flatten them all, to rid the Dwarven realm of the Aesir they held in a low regard, suddenly sounded like a dream, one that Astrid would never be able to see come true.

But then, she stood between a pair of otherworldly beings, the mist beginning to fade and shift away, and Astrid could hardly understand why she was there in the first place.

At first, there was: *Who am I?*

And then, swiftly, the next came like an onslaught upon her soul: *Why am I here? How could I have done this? Where did that farmer girl go? Where was she hiding?*

Astrid's eyes landed on Thor. *Is this what I get for loving a god?*

"Both of you," she growled, ripping one arm out of Loki's grasp, "get over yourselves. The Dwarven guard approaches, and I'd sooner see you both left to them if you *dare* keep this up!"

---

1. Translation: Cursed tongue.

The gods eyed each other again before Thor staggered, falling upon her weakly once more. Astrid tightened her grip across his waist, slipping down the path Sigyn once led, and falling into the shadows, where they were all left to their roaring thoughts, and nothing else.

"Everything we came to do hangs in the balance."

Sigyn stood on the threshold of an abandoned shack, her magic lingering and echoing around her hands. They lingered on the outskirts of Storby, where Ivaldi's guard presence grew thin. A symbol burnt into the rotten wood, still simmering from when Sigyn's fingertips dragged along it. The rune smoldered and hissed as the magic settled in. For a short time, the shack would remain hidden, buried beneath a cloak of shadow, only revealing itself to Ullr—that is, if he managed to find their location in the first place.

"Do not act as if you suddenly care about our mission," Astrid snapped. She dragged an old rag along Thor's arms, streaks of dried golden blood lingering across his skin. Somehow, his blood still glimmered within the dim firelight. "I will not defend the prince, but—"

Sigyn's laugh came out sharp and haggard, like a falcon. Her quick steps clapped against the floor as she stalked toward Astrid, the power still not leaving her hands. "But you will honor him all the same!" She pointed accusingly at the prince. "We have learned about the Vanir's presence in Svartalfheim, and the *Aesir Prince* has revealed his drunken self to the entire realm!"

Thor's breath caught from where he leaned against the wall. He could barely hold his eyes open, the ale leaving him slumped and exhausted. But—*how am I surprised*—it was the mention of the Vanir that brought forth his consciousness?

"The Vanir," he murmured. "In Svartalfheim…"

Sigyn's growl rocked through the shack as her magic accelerated her forward with an otherworldly speed. There was a gust of wind, dust furling through the air, and Sigyn loomed over Thor's slumped figure, talons gripping onto his hair. One hand snatched his jaw, silver nails piercing his immortal skin and drawing a thin line of golden blood.

"You wish to see every last one of us killed, don't you?" Her whisper was fervent, desperate. It sent a shudder down Astrid's spine. Never before had the sorceress seemed so vulnerable.

But, Astrid realized, the look in Sigyn's eyes had not been bred out of fear. The softness that overtook her was one of someone in love, someone who held something close to their chest, something that could be taken away.

Thor's head remained lazily against the wall. There was a moment of silence before a smile tugged at his mouth. "Forgive me, sorceress," he cooed. "For I did not realize you were a coward."

Sigyn's shriek ripped out of her throat.

One hand, her dominant one, Astrid knew, rose above her head. Magic brewed within her palm, spreading across the length of her fingers before culminating into a burst of untamed energy. It burned bright and silver, like the color of the sorceress's eyes.

Something, then, disappeared from Astrid. Perhaps it was the last shred of her light, the piece of the girl she once was that managed to remain, hiding in her soul's trenches. Whatever it was, it was gone. The moment Astrid realized Thor was about to be struck, it was taken. Besides, she had taken an oath, hadn't she?

"By the root of Yggdrasil, I will be the sword and shield of the house of Odinson."

In the end, there was only one way that Astrid knew how to love: *violently.*

Astrid's short blade whistled as she whipped it from her belt. The metal looked dark and muddled within the shadows, still stained with Dwarven blood. She pressed the edge against the nape of Sigyn's neck.

"You tread too far, sorceress," Astrid whispered.

Sigyn's eyes never left Thor. "A mortal bargaining her life for a god. A *tragic* story."

"Step *back*!" The blade sank through skin for a split second, and Astrid breathed in a rush of divinity, the confidence in her rising foolishly. "You'll have to kill me to get to him."

"Don't you hear yourself?" *Loki.* "This damned idiot has just about ruined everything. The Vanir will surely know we have arrived." He rushed forward, jerking Astrid's arm away from his wife. The sorceress staggered backwards, fingertips grazing where the incision just was. Loki's gaze was stunningly purple, shimmering like a pair of freshly plucked amethysts. Something was pleading about his expression, as if he were on his knees.

"We must retreat," he muttered. "Retreat to Asgard."

Astrid's head shook. "The hammer—"

"Has practically already made it into the Vanir's hands." Loki's shoulders sagged, his next words coming out in a hushed whisper that only she could hear. "The prince would listen to you. Tell him we need to leave."

"Why should we run from the Vanir? There isn't an enemy the Aesir can't—"

Loki's hands tightened like shackles around her arms. "You are as much of a fool as he! Ignorant and simply a *fool*." He allowed his voice to rise, catching the attention of Thor on the other side of the room. "The longer we remain, the more danger we are in. The All-Father will be merciful if we return empty-handed. He is just. He understands that the Vanir are—"

"Perhaps," Thor's voice echoed through the shack like an owl, "my father would be merciful." As his head rose, his drunken red eyes glowed a brilliant silver, storms brewing in the iris. "*I* am anything but."

Astrid managed to survive many things in her life. The Prince of Asgard was not, and probably never would be, one of them.

Pulling herself from Loki's grasp, she reached for Thor like it was an instinct, curving beneath his arm and hooking across his back. By the time she looked back toward Sigyn and Loki, Thor leaned against her side, drifting in and out of consciousness.

"We remain in Svartalfheim," Astrid said, and turned away as fast as possible, not at all eager to see the look upon their faces.

Astrid tucked around a corner, where a hallway or staircase might have once been, but no longer existed. She lowered Thor to the ground slowly, listening to him groan as his back finally hit the floor. Before she had the chance to grab the rag, Thor's warm and clammy hand wrapped around her wrist. Lazy kisses were pressed against her fingers, her knuckles, over each scar and stain of death.

"Dear Shadow," he murmured against her hand. "My beloved, how am I to even walk without you to guide me?"

Astrid rolled her eyes and tried to yank her hand away, but his grip grew cold and tight. "Be serious," she whispered. "You should be more careful, Thor. Drinking Dwarven mead? How can you be so..."

He yanked till she fell against his chest, her heart hammering against his own. "Do not scold me now, Shadow," Thor spoke against her mouth. "Let me bask in you."

Astrid wanted to melt and sink into his skin but held herself back. The guilt clung to her like sweat, and it was driving her mad. Where was she supposed to put her remorse when he only pressed it further into her soul?

"Have you seen what my devotion to you does?" Astrid pushed herself off his chest. "How it drives me away from my friends?"

Thor's brow rose in amusement. "I do not understand why it bothers you so. What is Loki to you, if not a pest nagging at your ear?"

"He is my friend."

"The creature is your god," Thor snarled, the drunkenness leaving him for a moment. "Gods are not your playthings."

"Then what are you?"

His hands clasped around her wrists like shackles. "Your keeper."

Panic raced beneath her skin. *How did I get here?* The world went blurry around her, the shack in Svartalfheim fading to become a quiet farmhouse, a wide field just waiting out the door. Astrid grew suffocated with nostalgia and yearning, desperate to return to the life that had been stolen from her, to escape from the clutches of the love of her life.

"Don't you see?" she whispered, her voice cracking beneath the growing fear. "Loving you has a consequence. One that refuses to leave me."

A sickening smile tugged at his lips. "Took the words right out of my mouth."

Astrid fervently tried to rip her hands out of his grasp, but he was unmoving, stronger than time itself.

"You love me," he murmured. "You *love* me."

Astrid found herself nodding, unable to deny it even if she wanted to. Where would she be without him? In a ditch, she knew, somewhere. In a grave, in Nifelheim, beloved and forgotten. Devotion and love, muddled to the extent that they blurred, and Astrid was left to believe they were the same.

She shuddered beneath his touch. "I do not wish to love you."

Thor's head tilted as he reached for her, his hand gentle and kind against the curve of her cheek. "I do not remember giving you a choice."

The words remained at the forefront of her mind as nighttime overtook Svartalfheim. The land of mines and labyrinths had a peculiar creature fluttering about during the late evening, wings snapping like a bat and chittering like a swift. It was like a lullaby as Astrid sat beside Thor's snoring figure, the mead and ale still lingering on the tip of his tongue. Murmurs echoed out from the front of the abandoned shack they found refuge in, Loki and Sigyn surely discussing the misgivings of their leader and his loyal shadow.

When Astrid's eyes fluttered shut, it was not from exhaustion or tiredness or even the need for slumber. It was her only way out.

The dream began in Thor's golden chambers. His bed was as wide as the farmhouse she used to call home, a canopy bed erected in the exact middle. Fur blankets and satin clothes rested across their skin as they lazily stretched out together, legs entangled and hands roaming. Thor threw the covers over their heads, only the morning dewy light streaming in from his windows managing to sink into their small hiding spot.

"What a divine creature," Thor murmured. His eyes clung to Astrid's neck before he reached, long and warm fingertips flexing around the nape of her throat. Her pulse quickened as his fingers pressed into it, desire beginning to lace his eyes. "A divine creature."

Astrid hated how sheepish she became. "There is nothing divine about me."

"Is life not divine?"

"Never-ending life, perhaps."

Thor shook his head, his smile small and disappointed. "To live and to die," he whispered. "*That* is divine." He inched closer, his hand tightening across her neck. "Do you know why, little *kriger*, I hold you this way?"

Astrid shook her head and leaned into his touch.

"Your life is in my hands," he said. "That mortal string that the Norn holds over your head"—he squeezed— "lies in my grasp. It is mine now." Thor's gaze left her throat, finally searing against her own eyes. The hunger within them grew fiery and dangerous. "Do you trust me to keep it safe?"

Astrid could not speak, even if she wanted to. She was trapped as his hand became something like a chain clamping down across her throat, rendering her mute. Perhaps he was meant to look loving, but it was not at all what she saw. His smile grew heinous and treacherous as she sank through the bed, falling through an inky darkness before landing on a hard, coarse ground.

When Astrid opened her eyes again, the bedroom had gone.

Blue fires as deep as the ocean smoldered on the rooftops of farmhouses and barns. Bodies littered the fields where they grew wheat, blood sinking into the soil and tainting the roots. Cattle fled from their homes, following the river that struck through Herjan, all the way to the neighboring mountains. Everything the homesteaders in Herjan created faded away on a single night.

Astrid rose from the muddy ground, her chest already heaving. Everything she wished to forget rushed back to the surface as if it had just happened.

The massacre of Herjan.

The destruction of her home.

All at the hands of—

Trumpets sounded east of her. Astrid faced the barrage of horses, the sound of their clobbering footsteps hauntingly familiar. They were the Aesir gods, come to rid their land of any rumor of a usurper.

At the forefront of the party, the All-Father stepped down from his eight-legged steed, Sleipnir. In one hand, he held up a torch, the roaring blue flames crackling at the top. As he drew nearer, Astrid's gaze focused on his other hand, already knowing what would be there, but looking all the same.

A small head detached from its body dripped starkly red blood onto the grassy floor. Shock was trapped on the young face's expression, never to be removed or changed. Astrid stepped closer, though she already knew who the young girl once was.

"My sister," Astrid murmured. "My blood."

When she looked upon the All-Father once more, Astrid jerked back, realizing that it wasn't Odin the One-Eyed after all.

Thor held her sister's head in his hands, a maliciously cruel smile tugging at his lips. She shuddered as she staggered backwards, her will to fight fading away in an instant. A voice that sounded much like her own echoed in the clouds overhead, growing so loud it sank into her head.

"The blood on his hands drips onto yours."

A crash resounded through the small shack, ripping Astrid out from the depths of her nightmare. She jolted up from her spot against the wall, jerking backward when she realized Thor had a chain-like grip over her wrist. In the distance, where Loki and Sigyn hunkered down, the sound of a door slamming shut rippled through the shack. Voices were carried back to where they lay.

Ullr and Darrow returned.

NINE

Astrid stared down at the blank map and rubbed her eyes.

But no matter how many times she thought herself to be simply tired, or still plagued with sleep, the page did not change. The map they found back in Ivaldi's study had the Dwarf's handwriting all over it, incomprehensible notes scribbled along the margins. Where the map should've been, however, remained blank, a magical sheen glimmering against the papyrus.

"I don't understand," Astrid muttered as she flipped the page over for the millionth time. "The thing is blank. How are we to navigate the labyrinth if it is blank?"

Darrow, whose attire changed into something sleek and silver, approached her with a pompous air about him. He held up a hand to gather the attention of the grumpy and exhausted gods. "Did you truly believe Dwarves would simply have a map of their precious mines? We are territorial creatures, after all!"

From the shadows of the shack, Loki chuckled. "Says the Dwarf who is hardly a Dwarf."

"Miners laid claim to their labyrinth with a map," Darrow explained as he plucked the page out of Astrid's hands. "But, to keep thieves away from their prize, the pages are charmed to be rendered invisible, unless you are within the maze itself."

"Great," Astrid grumbled, looking over her shoulder toward her godly companions. "We will be blind till we can get in."

Thor pushed himself off the wall, arms crossed over his chest as he stood beside her. The drunkenness that once plagued him slipped away with the sleep they managed to take. "You two were gone for hours," he said, his chin nodding toward Ullr, who drew countless runes along his fingers with a nub of ash. "What did you find?"

Ullr retrieved something from within his ragged robes. It was a dark key made from an ebony iron, the dim firelight from their small furnace casting a shred of light upon it. Ridges scored the key's handle, a series of runes unrecognizable to Astrid, carved into it.

"It will unlock one of the many doors that lead into Ivaldi's labyrinth," Ullr said.

Thor's brow furrowed. "Many? How will we know which is the right one?"

"That's the trick, my friends." Ullr shrugged his shoulders nonchalantly. "There is no way to know."

Astrid's frustration mingled with a restless sleep as she snapped at them. "How do we know this isn't a trap?"

"A trap?" Ullr repeated. "Ivaldi knows not of our journey into his labyrinth."

Loki stepped forward, Sigyn close at his side. "It is not the Dwarf we should be worried about." He waved a hand over his face, purple mist beginning to spread out from his fingertips. As his eyes flashed into amethysts, the magic contorted to show a series of twelve silhouettes, each shaped differently. Some wore antlers as crowns, others did not need one to prove their inherent royalty.

"What is this magic, trickster?" Thor muttered as he watched the figures take shape.

"They are the Vanir." Loki blew against the mist, and it spread, the silhouettes growing larger, till they stood all around them in a tight circle.

Their faces, Astrid realized, were shrouded by the magic, not entirely visible to them within the shack. She reached for her throat, feeling as though the air had been ripped out from her very lungs. Even though it was simply the work of illusionary magic, Astrid could not stop the fear from crawling up her throat. The Vanir were the rival clan of gods that had been cast out of Asgard long before she was ever a glimmer in her mother's eye.

Thor bristled at the sight of them. "What of them?"

"They come to take Mjolnir off Ivaldi's hands. We have no way of knowing when they might be here, when they might come for their prize." Loki's hands lowered as the magic began to fade, the purple mist sinking onto the floor. "To venture into the labyrinths without knowing is a suicide mission. Who says they won't be around the corner?"

"Who says they won't be there at all?" Thor snarled in question. "I will not base our movements upon 'what ifs' or 'maybes.' The

All-Father has ordered us forward, and I do not plan on failing him again."

Astrid gulped. The failure to retrieve Odin's Tear still rested against her shoulders, even if Thor didn't know it. Her need to succeed and prove herself to her companions weighed upon her more than anything else.

"Let the Vanir come," she said, reaching for the hilt of her blade. "Trap or not, we will scrounge through the maze till we find our prize."

Thor's hand rested upon her shoulder. "My brave shadow."

"Your foolish shadow," Loki hissed. With a deep breath, he shouldered his pack and tightened the leather braces resting against his arms. "Let us go, then."

Sigyn's brow rose. "Now?"

"If the Vanir approach," he muttered, "we might as well meet them head on, won't we?"

Thor let out a bellowing laugh and followed suit. For the first time in a long time, he let his hand rest upon Loki's back like an old friend. "That's the spirit, trickster!"

As the company collected their things and followed Darrow, who could lead the way through Storby with his eyes closed, Astrid was the last to leave, shutting the door to the shack behind her. Sigyn's magic still lingered upon it, and the moment she stepped away, it disappeared, blending into the shadows instantly. Astrid gripped onto her quiver, her pale white bow catching her eye.

When she turned around, Sigyn stood there, waiting for her.

"You have a look on your face, farmer girl," the sorceress said as they followed the company.

Astrid breathed in deeply. "What look?"

"As if you've seen a ghost."

Her brow furrowed as the dream she had came rushing back. The longer she strayed in her mind, the easier it would be for her to act like she *had* seen a ghost. Always, the image of her young sister, Frey, being slaughtered by the Aesir lingered behind her eyes. Always.

"Perhaps I have," Astrid murmured.

Sigyn stuck close to her side. "You have seen the prince's recklessness firsthand, and yet, you *still* carry his word like a dutiful worshipper. Tell me: How does a mortal manage to be so ignorantly resilient?"

"Do you mean to say that not all gods are reckless, that they all care for the world around them?"

"On the contrary," Sigyn replied. "Most of us do. Even these dangerous Vanir you all fear."

Astrid pressed her lips together. "I had forgotten. You are related to them, aren't you?"

"Distantly." Sigyn had a faraway look on her face. "The difference between us and them, farmer girl, is where our power comes from. Thor, for example, relies upon worship to be powerful. The Vanir grow stronger from the World Tree."

"Why are you telling me this?"

"Because," she murmured, "you have every chance to stop Thor from going down the path I see him leaning toward."

"I cannot stop a god."

Sigyn stopped and snatched onto Astrid's wrist, halting her in her path. Her grip was cold and tight, but not entirely threatening. "It is words like that that make you weak," she whispered. "You hold the heart of a god in your hands, with the power to mold it to your will, but all you do is shape it into what he wants. Perhaps it is because you crave it all the same."

Astrid's chest heaved as she ripped herself out of the sorceress's grasp. "I am *sick* and *tired* of you all placing Thor's future in my hands. You think I do not see the evil creeping in on him? You think I do not grow afraid of it? In the end, as you all *love* to point out, I am nothing more than a mortal. If there is anyone who might change his path, perhaps it is the rest of his immortal brethren!"

"Don't you dare pretend to be a pathetic little girl."

Astrid breathed in sharply. *Hold your temper,* she told herself, as an unavoidable heat rose to her cheeks. One hand rested firmly against the handle of her blade. "*What*?"

"Do you think we cannot see your truth?"

"Sigyn."

"The same darkness that plagues the prince lies in your eyes, Astrid."

For a moment, she was stunted, almost taking a step backward. How long had it been since the sorceress had called her by name? She could hardly recall.

"Talk all you want about Thor and his encroaching evil," Sigyn continued. "Talk about how it frightens you. Talk about how you can't recognize him anymore. Go ahead. We'll sit back and watch the darkness swallow you all the same."

"What I might do," Astrid seethed, her voice shaking, "I do for the gods."

"You are surrounded by those very gods, and I'll tell you now that the blood you devote to us doesn't mean a damned thing. Admit it: you enjoy the darkness just as much as Thor does."

Astrid could not look at anything else but the dirty floor beneath her feet. Her eyes widened as the words sunk deep into her skin, leaving a mark against her very soul. To stare the truth in the face was much harder than being given a lie. The darkness she saw within her own reflection was not quiet; it was not small.

"No," Astrid finally said, the word pushed out through clenched teeth, merely a sharp sound within the silence.

"I won't judge," Sigyn whispered, the corner of her lip curling into an amused smirk. "*Much*."

Footsteps approached from ahead.

Loki stood in front of them, his hands reaching. "What's the holdup?"

"Nothing at all," Sigyn said as she took her husband's hand, her eyes holding onto Astrid till she was forced to turn the other way.

Astrid watched the pair walk ahead of her, and she followed after a moment. They held each other's hands tightly, not daring to let go of the other. Astrid looked down at her own hands. They were too stained with the lives of the innocent for someone to hold them like that. Too stained, too evil, too dark.

The words from her dream rushed back to her.

The blood on his hands drips onto yours.

The labyrinth had more doors than Astrid could count.

On the opposite side of Storby, where one of the mountainous walls was erected from the ground, reaching the chasm above, simply wooden doors lined its base. They were separated by an inch or two, each looking starkly identical. Guards loitered along the wall, carrying torches that smoldered with a red flame at the top. They went back and forth in front of the doors, armed with heavy axes and swords.

Darrow hunkered down behind a wagon, the rest of the company looming beside him. "The labyrinth is off limits at this time of night," he whispered. "We need to avoid the guards and pick a door."

"How do we know which one to pick?" Astrid asked, already retrieving the map from its spot on her belt.

"You do not," he replied with a shrug. "You simply pick."

Astrid pressed her lips together as she overlooked her company. "Those are some odds, Darrow."

His bright eyes glanced around. "D-Do you not believe me?"

"I would not call it a matter of belief, old friend," Ullr murmured as he pressed a reassuring hand to the Dwarf's shoulder. "We don't...we don't entirely have the *luckiest* of odds, do we?"

"Nonsense." Thor pulled out his spear, the tip shining despite the darkness all around them. "How can we be unlucky when we have our *lykkebringer*[1] to guide us?"

The eyes of the company fell upon Astrid with a staggering silence.

"Lucky charm?" she repeated with a huff. "When have I ever proven to be good luck?"

It was Loki who inched toward her that time, nudging her out from behind the wagon with the point of his elbow. "How else could a mortal last this long alongside gods, if you were not inherently lucky?"

Without waiting for an argument, Ullr tossed the key to her.

Astrid grumbled under her breath as she stepped out from their hiding spot. "I can think of plenty of reasons."

There were a few yards between them and where the labyrinth began. She stowed away her weapons and kept a tight hold on the key, the map clenched between her gloved fingers. The guards had just made their way past them, heading in the opposite direction. Their torchlight illuminated the doors as they walked, giving Astrid a quick glimpse of them. She kept her head lowered as she ran, her small steps barely making a sound upon the stone beneath her feet.

The doors were twice her size, the keyhole directly across from her gaze. Astrid reached the first door. The closer she came to it, the louder a hum became in her ears. It was like a low beating drum

---

1. Translation: Lucky charm.

at first, but as her fingers ran over the keyhole, the sound blared in her head, almost like an alarm. She jerked back and stepped to the next door.

Astrid.

She froze in front of the door.

Astrid.

Inching forward, she let her hand graze the keyhole.

You are dark, aren't you?

Astrid flinched away from it.

Coward. Evil coward. As bad as him. As bad as—

She shoved the key into the lock and leaned toward the door as it exhaled. "Keep your magic words to yourself," she whispered and twisted the key.

A gust of wind and dust unfurled from the seams of the door. Without even a push or a pull, it swept open within an instant. The key, stuck within the keyhole, could not be removed, even when she jerked with all her strength.

"Tell us again how you aren't our lucky charm," Thor said as he jogged up behind her, breathless and grinning.

She jerked on it again, frustration mounting. "I cannot get the key," she muttered.

Darrow appeared at her other side, resting his slender and cold fingers against her armored wrist. "Let the key be, Astrid," he said. "It returns to where it came from. We won't be needing it again."

Lowering her arm, Astrid peered into the echoing darkness that lay on the opposite side of the door. Machinery clapped and clanked from deep within the labyrinth, though the source of the sound remained unseen. The only light that managed to peer back at them was from the red-hot energy that flows within Svartalfheim's core.

Thor gestured to the door. "After you, lucky charm."

"Don't tell me you're going to start calling me that now."

"Tell me," he murmured in her ear, "Would you prefer that, or my shadow?"

Unable to answer with the lump forming in her throat, Astrid mumbled something incoherent to even her and stepped over the threshold of Ivaldi's treacherous labyrinths.

The moment they all stepped into the labyrinth, the door closed shut with a slam, without a hand to do so. The walls began to glow ominously, the red veins from the realm's core pulsing like a heartbeat all around them. Once the light grew bright enough for them to see, Astrid glanced around at their surroundings. The walls were narrow and pressed upon them without fail, the floor rising and falling as if it struck through a hilly region. Even as they stood there, without moving a muscle, Astrid could hear the corridors shifting and moving in the far-off distance.

Fear began to clasp down on her heart. The sounds were something a mortal was not meant to hear, she realized, as it echoed closer and closer. Without even knowing, the way ahead could be changed in a matter of seconds, and the idea almost forced her into a paralyzed fright. She raised her hands shakily to unfold the map, flattening the creases against her palm.

"By the Norn," she murmured.

Lines and curves began to slowly appear upon the map. They struck in all sorts of directions, turning and shifting with every passing minute. Once the entire page was full, they stayed the same, for the most part. Now and then, a corridor would move or even just fall away. Astrid traced the lines with her fingers, finding a spot in the middle where the labyrinth turned into a rounded cavity, a small hammer drawn within it.

"That's it!" Darrow appeared to her left, looming over her shoulder and pointing a painted fingernail at the center. "The Hall of Victories, as Ivaldi so humbly likes to call it. It is where he stores his creations before they are put to use."

Loki curved around them, his hand raised to show a brilliant plume of red fire at the center of his palm. He peered at the map with narrowed eyes. "What of Brokkr and Sindri? The Dwarves that guard it?"

"They would be at the entrance," Darrow replied. "Unless they have moved toward surveilling the maze themselves."

Astrid kept a tight hold onto the map as Thor shoved the others away.

"Hand it over, my shadow," he demanded, one hand already reaching for it.

She stared down at it. "I..."

"What?"

"I believe I can understand it."

Thor's brow furrowed as he looked at the map. "What makes you think I can't?"

"Give it a try."

He stared down at it before looking at the corridor in front of them. Once again, the walls shifted and moaned as the mine changed in the distance. Thor grunted irritably. "Tell me, Astrid, how *you* might understand what *I* cannot."

"Simple," she whispered, her eyes glued to the map.

It was oddly familiar to her, in a way she could not outrightly understand. What an outlandish thing to consider. How could she, a mortal Asgardian, understand a Dwarven map?

But perhaps it was not the map at all, or the geography within it. Rather, she understood it inherently, instinctively, as if it were something she was always meant to do. The Norn, the fate weavers who spent eternity caring for the roots of Yggdrasil, already planned for Astrid to be there, in that very moment, and bestowed upon her the knowledge needed to read it.

Her destiny stood a few feet ahead, and Astrid wanted to run in the opposite direction.

When she looked up from the map, her company huddled around, watching with puzzled expressions. It was only Loki, out of them all, who had the oddest glint in his eye.

Pride? No, it couldn't have been.

"Darrow and I can lead the way," Astrid said. "You can read it, can't you?"

"Well, I *am* the son of Marrow," he mumbled as he scratched the back of his head. "But how can *you* read it?"

"I-I...I'm not..."

Thor's hand on the back of her neck shut her up. "Fine, then," he said. Easy words, not fighting words. And yet, they brought a chill to Astrid's spine as his fingers tightened over her pulse. "Lead the way."

Astrid gulped and looked down at the map in her hands. The path ahead looked rather straightforward, as long as they could calculate when a corridor was about to shift. Luckily for them, Darrow managed to inherit the Dwarven instinct and could turn them a different way if need be.

"How can you tell?" Astrid asked once they had been walking for some time.

Darrow shrugged. "It is as if the walls of the labyrinth speak to me."

They continued through the labyrinth with lightened hearts. Darrow's ability to navigate the maze without the map brought an ease to Astrid, as she grew more and more nervous about her ability. The Dwarvish language was littered across the page, but it was the symbols—garish and rune-like—that caught her eye. She followed the feeling they gave, the inherent instinct that told her which way to turn.

"Perhaps you are blessed with a bit of the *dvergøye*[2] ." Darrow walked alongside her, his eyes clinging to the road ahead.

Astrid frowned.

"I don't suppose you know what that is, now do you?"

"Unfortunately," she murmured, her head angled over her shoulder to catch a glimpse of the party behind them, "I am not fluent in Dwarvish."

---

2. Translation: Dwarven eye.

"Well," Darrow explained, a slight skip in his step, "In your language, it roughly translates to the Dwarven Eye. It is the ability to see the ore veins in the walls, or understand the symbols crafted by my ancient ancestors."

The ore veins. Astrid glanced around the walls on either side of them. The pulsating red stood out to her like a sore thumb. They illuminated the path they took. But the gods took to carrying plumes of fire to see the way ahead. Not even the Aesir could see it, she realized.

"I am no Dwarf."

"No, but that does not mean you cannot still be blessed with it. How else would you be able to know the way ahead?"

Astrid glanced down at the map again. "I fear I know nothing," she whispered. "There is only a feeling, deep within me."

"You Asgardians have the Norn to thank for that, don't you?"

"Is there no fate weaver in Svartalfheim?"

Darrow laughed lightly, the sound echoing across the corridors. "We Dwarves uncover our own fate, you hear? Why else would I be a poet? Or, what is it you folk call it?"

"A skald."

He snapped his fingers and twirled, not even missing a step. "Then a skald is what I shall be."

Astrid couldn't remember the last time she felt so...normal. There was nothing divine about Darrow, except for his ability to pluck music out of the air like a mage. But no rays of golden light radiated off him. No power lay behind his words, no influence seeking to seep beneath her skin. He was simply a Dwarf who forged his path, regardless of what the Norn might've already foretold.

Pain and joy struck her at the same time.

Was that what it felt like to be mundane again?

To not be basked in the divinity of the Aesir?

Astrid tilted her head toward the humming Dwarf and opened her mouth to speak. *You are only a Dwarf,* she wanted to say, *but you have made me feel mortal again.*

But something upon the map caught her eye. She paused in their trek, unaware of how the corridor walls were beginning to shift around them.

"Why have we stopped?" Thor strode forward, his hand clasping against Astrid's shoulder. "What is the meaning of—"

"Something is wrong," Astrid murmured.

Beside her, Darrow's back hunched like a frightened cat. "I feel it," he whispered. "Something approaches."

The map began to change within her hands. The symbols that were once simply drawn with a pencil took on a threatening shade of red. The borders followed suit, till they pulsed with a frightening power. Astrid felt herself beginning to tremble as a magnetic power reached out, threatening to grasp her by the throat.

"The map," she whispered.

The way forward grew muddled till it disappeared. The inky black lines shifted and changed. Words that were entirely known to her took shape within the center of the map. It was as if the maker loomed over her shoulder, a quill in one hand.

Astrid's eyes went wide.

I see you.

"Ymir's breath," she whispered before her voice rose to a shout. "It's a trap!"

Instantly, the corridor surrounding the company moaned as it shifted around. Darrow ripped the map out of her hands, the page tearing in half and falling to the floor.

"He has watched all along," Darrow murmured. He trembled with unmistakable fear. "Ivaldi has watched all along."

The sound of Thor's blade being ripped from the sheath sliced through the air, as though they were miners searching for silver. "My company," he shouted, sharp twitches of lightning bursting around his fingertips. "Take up arms!"

But it was far too late to make any such movements.

The labyrinth could keep outsiders away without the hand of a Dwarf involved. It had a mind of its own, built to protect its riches in any way possible. Even if it meant crushing them to the very ground they stood upon.

Astrid was reaching for her short blade when the ceiling shifted overhead, another wall falling upon them. She raised her head, watching as rocks and stones cascaded down upon them like rain. Hands grabbed onto her, jerking her in one direction as the ceiling fell on their heads.

And the labyrinth went dark.

TEN

“Open your eyes, farmer girl.”

Pain seared into her temple as the world returned around Astrid. The red veins within the walls grew brighter. Footsteps clicked on either side of her, in a circle. Repeating over and over again. She reached for her forehead and winced when her gloved hand pressed against a bloody gash.

“Careful, now.”

Astrid groaned slightly as arms hooked beneath her arms and hoisted her back onto her feet.

Loki stood in front of her, his grip tightening. “Are you well?”

“I-I...”

“*Astrid*.” Loki’s ebony eyes were wickedly wide, streaks of purple beginning to strike across the darkness. His fingers pressed painfully into her skin, growing stronger by the second. Perhaps it was fear, perhaps it was anger. “Are you well?”

She forced herself to nod. “I’m fine,” she mustered.

Loki’s shoulders relaxed slightly.

“Are you angry?”

“Angry?” He scoffed, a sharp laugh filling the dusty corridor. “Angry could not begin to describe it, farmer girl.”

Astrid breathed in deep, struggling to find her voice. "I am sorry," she whispered. "I should have read the map better, I should have noticed—"

"You believe I am angry with you?"

She avoided his stare. "What else is there to be?"

"The fury I feel," he seethed, his voice trembling, "lies with the man who brought us here in the first place."

"Loki—"

"We have been split up," Loki snarled, releasing his hold on her. "A wall separates us from the rest of our company."

Astrid blinked a few times, pulling herself out of the dizziness that came from her wound. Leaning against one of the walls, Darrow had his head in his hands. The Dwarf might not have been used to such violence, not used to seeing blood and bruises line his slender fingers.

"Hold your head up, skald," Astrid called out to him, and he shakily raised his eyes to her. "We are all fine and well, alright?"

He nodded numbly but did not speak.

Astrid strode towards the Dwarf and knelt at his feet. When he did not look at her still, she reached into a pocket around her belt and retrieved the braid of sandy-blonde hair she kept on her person.

Darrow's eyes caught onto it curiously. "What's that?"

"This braid once laid on my sister's shoulder," Astrid whispered as she laid it on his palm. "She faced all the things a young child should never know. And when her life was taken, I took a piece of her strength with me. Can you feel it?"

He blinked. "Feel what?"

"Her strength."

Darrow stared down at the coarse hair, his thumb trailing over the pattern absentmindedly. After a few quiet moments, his brow furrowed tightly. "Yes," he murmured. "I believe I can." With a sad smile, he placed the braid back in her hands. "I am sorry for your loss."

"Don't be," she whispered. "She haunts me still."

Emotion began to clutch at Astrid's throat, so she stood and slipped the memento back in her pockets. When she went to look at the path ahead, her eyes caught onto the trickster. His stare bore into her for a second longer than she expected, before he pulled away.

The corridor in which they were traveling was changed into something new. On one side, a new wall was erected between them and the rest of their party. On the other, there were three tunnels before them. Each echoed into darkness, each smelling fouler than the last. The way forward, now, was muddled with shadows.

Loki stood in front of the unmovable wall, one hand pressed against it.

"We must keep moving," Astrid said. She walked toward the Dwarf and grabbed onto his wrist, gently tugging him back onto his feet. "Come forth, skald. You may be our only hope in finding a way out of here."

Darrow gazed up at her. "What more can I do when I failed to see the trap before our eyes?"

"I was blind to it all the same," Astrid murmured. "Does that make me lesser to you?"

"No."

"Then we continue forth. The only thing left for us is to rectify what we have lost." Astrid forced him to stand up straight. "You may be our skald, but you are a piece of our company, now. Lead us to the hammer, and you will have your time in glory."

Darrow watched her quietly before standing straight on his own. The musical glint returned to his eye as he reached into his robes, retrieving a leather-wrapped book and a stick of lead. "You are quite the wordsmith yourself, Asgardian."

Ignoring the sheepish blush that threatened to pull across her cheeks, Astrid turned back to Loki and snatched onto his arm. "That includes you, trickster. We mustn't linger any longer."

Loki pressed his hand to the wall. His eyes were cloudy and dark, his magic curling around his fingers. "My beloved lies on the other side of this wall," he murmured.

"Do not tell me you fear for the life of your sorceress."

Angry eyes shot toward her. "That sorceress carries my heart. Tell me, why am I not to fear for her?"

"If we have been split up," she hurriedly whispered, "Sigyn lies in the company of our prince. He will protect her."

"Blind farmer girl."

Her eyes narrowed. "Loki."

"You cannot see that *he* is why I am afraid." The trickster god pushed himself away from the wall. "All hope for finding the weapon lies with you, skald." Those deadly eyes found the Dwarf. "Lead the way forth, or we may all succumb to Ivaldi's labyrinth."

Darrow faced the three paths ahead. He drew in a deep breath before raising his chin and smelling the air. His thin brow furrowed the longer he stared. After a moment, his shimmering eyes found the way ahead.

"Follow me," he said, his voice surprisingly strong.

The trio went through the path on the right. Light came from a flame resting in Loki's palm, while Astrid and Darrow followed the pulsing energy from the red veins in the walls. Nothing made sense about the road that they took. All of it, to Astrid, looked rather the same, and it began to drive her down a pit of insanity. Somewhere, within it all, lay a small cavity where Mjolnir would be resting. Perhaps there would be a pair of legendary Dwarves guarding it, or perhaps there wouldn't be.

All of it hung in the air, and it made Astrid want to climb out of her very skin.

Astrid stepped alongside the Dwarf, Loki's presence dark and grueling from behind her. A deadly heat radiated off him, one that Astrid had not felt for quite a long time.

"Tell us, Darrow," she called out, "stories of old while we march."

Darrow smiled sheepishly. "I am afraid I know little of olden stories."

"How about the one you plan to write about us?"

"This would be the brilliant climax, wouldn't it?" Darrow murmured as his eyes took on a faraway look. The walls were growing thinner around them, a smell that was only found deep in the core of Svartalfheim engulfing them, the air becoming less and less with every step. "Where the heroes face their foe, where the cowardly show their strength, where the bard is far more than a bard."

"I suppose so." Astrid glanced at the Dwarf. She was no mystical creature, and yet, she could feel the fear touching her skin. "Have you found a name for it yet?"

Darrow's eyes lit up within the darkness. "Well, *yes*, actually. Do you wish to hear it?"

She nodded and glanced over her shoulder. Loki drew nearer, his attention grabbed despite his unwillingness to show it.

"I shall call it, 'The Warrior and her Divine.'"

Astrid stopped in her tracks. "What?"

"D-Did I not say it loud enough?" Darrow frowned as his confidence began to fade. "Do not tell me you do not like it."

"I hardly understand," she whispered. "I thought you were writing your tale about our search for Mjolnir. Of the Aesir."

Darrow shrugged. "That's exactly right."

"But—"

Loki stepped around her, the corner of his lip tugging into the smallest of smiles. "Something tells me," the trickster whispered, "that the skald's story might, in fact, be about *you*, farmer girl."

"Rightly so." Darrow continued walking without a care. "A tale of love and death, of a mortal within a god's world." He raised his chin, rather proud of himself. "Exciting, isn't it? Everyone loves a story about a mortal amidst the unimaginable."

Astrid walked behind them like a ghost without direction. Stories were not written about simple Asgardians, simple warriors who barely made a mark upon Yggdrasil when compared to her godly companions. It was the time of the gods, not the time of man.

"You'd write a story," she murmured, "about *me*?"

Darrow paused in his trek to look over his shoulder at her. "What's the matter?"

"Nothing," she blurted, but that was a lie. Her eyes were stuck on the floor.

"My little farmer girl," Loki murmured as he came to her side. The warmth of his magic tickled her frail skin. "That damned prince has ruined you."

"This has nothing to do with—"

"You cannot recognize your own power while standing in his light." The trickster hooked a finger around her chin, like he always did. "*Min elskede venn*[1], when will you see what I see?"

As she looked at him, Astrid was overwhelmed with the urge to bite at his fingers like a caged animal. The line between shame and rage grew blurry. She ripped herself from his grasp, baring her teeth like the wolf she knew herself to be.

Loki let his hand drop, his head tilting with pity.

Pity.

Astrid leaned in, her voice dark and defensive. "I see the creature that I am," she hissed. "Tell me, trickster, what do you see?"

---

1. Translation: My beloved friend.

He only stared, lips parted but the words were trapped within.

Darrow called out from a few paces ahead. "This way, my companions! I believe we have uncovered the Hall of Victories."

Ducking around the trickster god, Astrid stayed low as she approached Darrow. He peered around a corner and nodded his chin with an excited glimmer in his eyes. Astrid looked around him. The Hall of Victories sat at the end of a corridor; a rounded entryway littered with sharply carved runes that glowed ominously within the darkness. There was no door blocking the entrance, or even a guard positioned in front of it. It was eerily quiet, a windy draft pulling them forward.

Astrid, suddenly, felt sick to her stomach. "This does not feel right," she whispered. "Where are the guards? The Dwarves you warned us of?"

Darrow shrugged. "Wouldn't this be a good thing?"

"There should be something blocking our way," Astrid said as Loki came up alongside her. "Unless it is another trap."

"Even if it is," Loki said, "would you be willing to turn away from it?"

Astrid peered over her shoulder at him. There was no telling what lay ahead, though the stirring in her chest told her exactly what it might be. If Ivaldi knew they had the map and managed to trap them within his labyrinth, what was to say that giving them the easy way forward was also a trap itself? Perhaps they were to stumble into another cage, one that would be impossible for them to break out of. There was only *one* god amongst them, after all.

"No," Darrow replied instead. "Right?"

Astrid smiled at him, though she could hardly feel it. "Right, skald. We will see to it that your story has a bountiful ending."

The Dwarf beamed from ear to ear.

Astrid stepped around the corner and drew her blade. Upon either side of her, Darrow and Loki took up arms, though the poet merely carried a minuscule dagger. The Hall of Victories was before them, and they were ready to face it head-on.

Amber fires were roasting upon torches within the hall. It was not a long room at all, but rather rounded and hidden, like a secret room within a place of worship. Ornate artwork done in gold lined every bit of the walls, showing the countless legends surrounding the Dwarves of Svartalfheim. And, in the very middle, there was a canopy that reached the ceiling, a case beneath it. The glass case was left wide open as Astrid inched closer, her eyes widening as she looked upon the pedestal. A velvet pillow sat at the top, an indent upon the middle where a heavy hammer once was laid to rest.

Once.

"It isn't here," Astrid whispered.

She reached for where it was, her fingers just barely touching the pedestal, when short footsteps came from behind them.

"Tell me, mortal. Did you *truly* think it would've been?"

The trio whipped around, their weapons raised.

Standing within the entryway of The Hall of Victories was a creature Astrid only recognized from storybooks. There was little to be said about the Vanir within Asgard, besides that they were the Aesir's other halves, their rivals, and inherent enemies. According to legend, the mere blood of the Aesir would boil beneath their skin when they came too close to the Vanir. Astrid glanced to her right, where Loki stood.

The trickster, who was rarely one to show fear, watched the creature before them with unsettling wide eyes. He twitched and trembled, flickers of pain showing itself across his aged face.

She had never seen him in such a state before. It drove a determination through her, sparking a heated anger that was too loud to ignore. Once, Astrid was burdened with the idea of taking over her family farm, of protecting everything her father built with his bare hands. It was stripped away in the dead of night, and she vowed to protect all things she held close to her heart. And suddenly, as the deadly creature loomed over them, Astrid wished to cover the god with her mortal body. How many times had he protected her in the past? She lost track long ago.

Astrid turned to the god, one hand already stretching across Loki's chest. "Who are you?" she asked in a low voice.

The god's skin was as bronze as the walls surrounding them, the firelight glistening against him. Pale hair rolled down his back in waves. Strikingly green eyes, as green as fresh dew on the fields in the early morning, stared down at her with an unbelievable heaviness. The god did not smile, the god did not frown. He merely stared.

"I am Freyr," he said, his voice as strong as the oldest tree. "Brother of Freyja, the beloved queen of my people."

Loki stepped forward. "Svartalfheim is no place for the Vanir."

"I could say the same of you, Aesir," Freyr murmured. He left the entryway and delved deeper into the Hall of Victories.

Astrid's attention got pulled into the other artifacts and prizes stowed away within cubbies carved into the golden walls. They shimmered as the god strode by them, not paying any mind to all the power resting on either side of him.

His armor shone as bright as the sun, almost making it impossible for him to be looked at. A magnificent blade hung from his belt, the tip almost dragging against the floor below. A crown fashioned from antlers rested upon his head, his breastplate decorated similarly.

Freyr's eyes fell upon Astrid once more. "You have not answered me, mortal. Did you believe the weapon would have been here?"

She was speechless for far too long. When had she ever encountered a Vanir god before? *Never,* she told herself. *And those who have, did not live long enough to tell the tale.*

Loki moved to shield her with his broad frame. "A weapon of such magnitude should lie in the hands of the All-Father." He brandished Laevateinn, his scepter. Without even uttering a word, the shimmering gem at the top began to glow. "Where have you taken Mjolnir?"

"As far as I am concerned," Freyr said, "the hammer has been rightfully sold. It belongs to the Vanir. Does that frighten you?"

"*Nothing* frightens me."

A foggy image of Loki began to appear behind the Vanir. It grew sharper as the seconds went by. The trickster was a master of illusion, a shapeshifter capable of manipulating whatever he pleased. The figure appearing behind the Vanir was not entirely

Loki himself, but rather a piece of him. The copy began to draw a blade, the tip inching closer to Freyr's broad neck.

Freyr's lip curved upwards. "Your mystics do not go unnoticed by me, trickster." With an indescribable speed, the Vanir's sword came free from its sheath and sank into the foggy image behind him.

Loki hissed and stumbled backwards, pressing in upon Astrid. "*Røm herfra*," he whispered out of the corner of his mouth. "*Flykte!*"

The words he spoke were jumbled in her head: *Escape from here. Flee!*

But before she had the chance to argue, the trickster flung himself forward, magic bursting out from the tip of his scepter. A dozen Lokis popped into existence all around them, running toward the Vanir without a moment to lose. They swarmed in upon Freyr, almost looking like they were about to overtake him from where Astrid stood. Exhilaration pumped through her chest. Beside her, Darrow held up his short blade.

Suddenly, they felt like heroes within his story.

"*Fool.*"

Freyr moved and looked like a ray of light. His sword sliced through each illusion instantly, the blade barely making a sound as it soared through the air. Amidst it all, the real Loki ducked and parried, but it was far too late to fight back.

The edge of Freyr's blade sliced along Loki's side, diving through his armor as though it were made from wool. The trickster skidded backwards, his teeth gritted together so hard that veins were beginning to grow from beneath his skin. He staggered into Astrid's arms, both of them hitting the pedestal before crumbling to the ground.

Loki's groan filled the air, touching her in a way she never expected. His eyes still held a tint of purple within them, his scepter glowing despite its master's power beginning to fade. There was a gash at his side, far deeper than any mortal-made sword could have done. But he was a god fighting another god, and their weapons were more than capable of ridding the other of their immortality.

"Do not..." Loki whispered through his teeth. "Do not..."

Astrid knew not what he wanted to say. Perhaps he would tell her not to fight, or it would be the opposite, making sure that she would not stand down.

But she was barely paying attention.

Golden blood fell from his side like a river, already dripping onto her hands. The breath hitched in the back of her throat as the divinity began to sink through her armor, and down beyond her skin. It coursed through her veins like a disease, like an irreversible sickness. Astrid rose from the god's side, feeling as though she held the reins of another's body, her mortal one still lying against the floor.

Astrid caught a glimpse of her reflection in the wall as she faced the Vanir. Starkly maroon hair flowed around her narrow face like a veil. Where she was once gaunt and malnourished from travel became fleshed out and full. Strength returned to her arms, to her legs, to her very heart. Even in the reflection, she could see the gold beneath her skin, radiating from the inside out, just like it did with her godly companions.

A goddess.

Astrid brandished her blade and ran toward Freyr.

Every step felt more powerful than the last. She was unstoppable, unbeatable, unbreakable.

That is, until she reached the Vanir.

Freyr's armored hand snapped out the moment she was before him. His gauntlet clasped around her neck and lifted her off the ground. Astrid's eyes went wide as the realization hit her, the blade she carried clattering against the floor.

I am no goddess.

I am breakable.

"Silly mortal," Freyr said, his eyes narrowing pitifully. "Unlike yours, my blood does not fade."

Beneath his grasp, Astrid drew in gulps of air as his armor sliced through her tender skin, staining him with scarlet.

In his other hand, Freyr readied his legendary blade. "My sword will forever remember your blood, Asgardian," he murmured. "If that is any consolation."

Astrid never thought about how she might face death one day. Most Asgardian warriors perished in battle and awaited the Valkyrie's call to take them to the halls of Valhalla. But, somehow, at that very moment, Astrid had the growing sense that that was not her destiny. Perhaps the Norn gave her a glimpse of the string they weaved, the one that stretched long and far, the one that reflected her mortal life.

She saw it quiver, like her bowstring.

And then, suddenly, it *tightened.*

"Unhand her!"

Darrow shot to the god's side, his short dagger shrieking as it met the brunt of Freyr's indestructible armor.

Astrid's widened eyes trailed down to the Dwarf.

No, she thought, she screamed, she pleaded. *Do not risk your life for me.*

But Freyr's attention was already pulled. His hand released from around her throat, and her feet hit the ground with a *bang.* Astrid collapsed as tremors rolled up to her knees, rendering her incapable of walking for a split second.

A split second.

And that was all it took.

Freyr's blade soared through the air before it found its mark in Darrow's chest. He raised the sword, and the Dwarf sank against the iron, an unbearable expression forever trapped on his slender face.

"Pity," Freyr murmured. He lowered the sword, and Darrow fell off the edge like a doll. When his back hit the ground, inky blood was already spreading to Astrid's feet like reaching hands.

Astrid crawled like a child. Her hands cupped the Dwarf's face. She shook him, squeezed, and pinched. *You risked your life for me.* She slammed her palm against Darrow's cheek.

Fool! Slap.

Idiot! Slap.

Stupid! Slap.

Tears streamed down her cheeks. How could she weep for a creature she barely knew? Perhaps it was because he never wrote his story, he hadn't risen to fame, and he hadn't proven himself. Perhaps it was because he saw her as the hero of his tale.

The Warrior and her Divine.

Astrid raised her tear-stricken face to find Freyr. A guttural scream erupted from her throat. Within the Vanir, she saw them all: Thor, Loki, Sigyn, Ullr. Every one of them, blessed with eternal life, when the ones like Darrow would simply sink at the mere sliver of bravery.

How?

Why?

She screamed again, the sorrow turning into something she could hardly recognize.

Freyr crouched in front of her with a tilted head, as if he watched a child. "I have seen your soul," he murmured. "Sword-slayer, perhaps. But you are plagued." He rose back up. "You weep and you are weak."

The Vanir turned toward the entryway to The Hall of Victories as a pair of silhouettes appeared. He passed them by, only stopping to utter a few words, not even taking another look at those he left behind.

"Kill them."

ELEVEN

T he scream that came next was not of sorrow.

The pair of Dwarves stepped into The Hall of Victories, long maces and double-edged axes waiting in their hands, like executioners. They were far larger than the average Dwarf, their power rendering them incapable of being simple miners. Astrid's eyes found them during her wails, their feet slamming against the marble floor ringing like a war drum. Confusion crossed her at first; they did not dress like the other guards or wielded the same weapons. They were far too large, far too gruesome, as if they hadn't stepped outside the labyrinth in centuries.

The one on the right, twin maces dangling from his large hands, stepped forward. "*Kriger,*" the Dwarf exclaimed, "you meet your demise at the end of the legendary Brokkr and Sindri's blades. Aren't you honored?"

Beside him, Sindri grinned and panted like a dog.

Astrid's eyes grew wide as Darrow's first words from the tavern rushed back to her. They were the Dwarves said to watch over the labyrinth. Stories foretold them to be nothing more than weapons, master blacksmiths who trailed behind their master, Ivaldi, like loyal and spineless dogs. Their armor did not fit them, it was far too small or far too big. The real power lay in their hands, hands that have built weapons capable of striking a god from the sky.

But Astrid no longer sat before them as a woman, as an Asgardian, as a mortal. Her rage was forged in fire; it swallowed words and spat them out as a blade. Nothing was left untouched within her. Everything was lit with roaring flames, and she was ready to watch all the Nine Realms burn down.

Perhaps that was all it took. A single thing, a single strike, a single match.

That was all it took to start an unbeatable fire.

Astrid snatched her blood-soaked blade from the ground and rose to her feet. Her clothes, her armor, her hands, her hair—all of it was stained with Darrow's essence. His spirit remained still, upon her very being, and she was in no rush to set him free. She would wear him like a cloak, she would braid him into her hair, she would tattoo him against her fragile skin. The skald was dead, perished at the hands of the gods, like everything else.

Like everything else.

Brokkr came first. He wielded a pair of twin maces, their spikes glinting with untouched silver. His steps pounded against the floor as he approached, shaking the very walls around them.

Astrid slammed the hilt of her blade against her chest rhythmically, not once feeling the pain. "*For Odin,*" she chanted. "*For Darrow!*"

She shot forward like a berserker. Astrid leapt onto the pedestal that once held the hammer, kicking herself off it as though she carried a Valkyrie's wings. The blade twisted around in her palm till the pointed edge was pointed downwards.

Brokkr roared, a Dwarvish war cry unknown to her Asgardian ears ringing through the small room. His maces crossed in front of him defensively.

She landed upon his chest and gripped onto his weapons, keeping them locked in the position he branded them in. Her sword sank through his chest, dipping between the gaps of his poorly fitted armor. It plunged deeper and deeper, till the other end erupted out from his spine, her knuckles pressing against his opened wound. Brokkr fell backwards, and she remained upon him like a spider. Astrid lifted the blade and plunged it again. When she did it a third time, blood as black as midnight splattered across her face.

Sindri released an ear-shattering howl as he tackled Astrid to the floor. Smaller than his companion, Sindri relinquished his weapon and slammed her back into the ground, claw-like hands gripping onto her shoulders. Talons squeezed through her leather armor and punctured the skin beneath. A hungry look passed over the Dwarf's face. He lifted and slammed her down another time, listening to the sound of her head cracking against the golden floor below.

Astrid's hands skidded around till her fingers wrapped around the hilt of her sword. She kept her eyes focused on Sindri as the brunt of the blade sank into his chest. Astrid gritted her teeth and pushed it further, till it felt as though her hand might grip onto his beating heart.

Black blood dripped from Sindri's parted lips and trickled across her face, curving down her cheek like a deadly tear.

"Look at me," she hissed. "Look at the weapon you have succumbed to."

The Dwarf died against her chest.

Astrid shoved the unmoving creature to the side. For a moment, she could only lie there. Even when there was a rush of steps from the entryway, murmurs in the Dwarvish language reaching her ears, Astrid remained still. Some of it she could hear, some of it she could understand.

"Beast…killer…Swordslayer."

Pieces from the ceiling began to crumble, clattering to the ground beside her head. Perhaps it was a defense mechanism Ivaldi built into his labyrinth. The Hall of Victories could collapse at the sign of an intruder, taking the enemy along with the riches stowed within.

In the end, she could hardly care.

There was no sorrow left for her to give. Only anger lived in her, only rage.

It wasn't until hands curled around her arms, dragging her out of the way of a large boulder from the ceiling.

Loki groaned through his pain and hooked his hands beneath her arms, hoisting her up and pushing her back against the wall. Astrid struggled against his touch as her thoughts ran amok in the back of her head, not daring to give her one semblance of peace.

You are an ugly creature. The blood on your hands stains him.

Astrid's hands flattened against his chest and shoved.

The god stumbled, his eyes wild and lit with fury. Despite the wound at his side, he shot forward with a paranormal speed, his golden bloodstained hands pressing her shoulders into the wall behind her.

"Snap out of your haze," he said and gripped onto the wound at his side.

Astrid tried to meet his eye but grew sick at what she saw. The god who once called her farmer girl, the god who once believed hope remained within her still, could no longer look at her in the same light. There was a disgust hidden there, just waiting to be set free.

"Leave me," she whispered. "I know it is what you want."

Loki snarled something she could not understand under his breath before snatching onto her shoulder. "Do not pretend you are the weak farmer girl from Herjan," he hissed. "I have seen you, and I love you still. Can you hear me?" He shook her like a madman, eyes wickedly wide. "I have seen you, and I love you still."

Astrid shuddered. "I cannot look at you," she whispered.

"Why?"

"Your eyes reflect me in a terrible way."

Loki's face contorted in a way she had never seen before. He pressed his lips together so hard the color drained from his face. And, suddenly, he reached, wrapping his arm across her shoulders and holding her against his chest. He held her there, in a hug, she realized, for a moment, while The Hall of Victories collapsed all around them.

Astrid fought the urge to sink, to fade into his skin and never leave.

When he pulled away, he rested his forehead against her own, one hand gripping the back of her neck. Most warriors did such a thing after a battle. It was a symbol of companionship, of a brotherhood. Astrid sighed and grabbed the back of his neck in the same fashion.

"*Min elskede venn*," Astrid whispered. "Why can't you let me die?"

"For I have seen your thread, and it is far from spent." He stepped back and reached for her. "Take my hand, Astrid."

She looked back down at Darrow's body, the rocks beginning to fall upon him like a tomb. Astrid reached desperately, searching for anything she might take. Somewhere in her armor was the braid she plucked from her sister's body, and she couldn't leave till she had something from him, too. She couldn't.

Within his cloak, Astrid retrieved a leather-bound notebook, no bigger than the palm of her hand. A "D" was carved into the middle, ornate and flamboyant.

Darrow.

Astrid tucked the book within her armor and took the trick-ster's hand.

Ivaldi always wanted them to escape the labyrinth.

At least, that was the conclusion Astrid made as she and Loki burst through the door and back into the echoing evening of Svartalfheim. The trickster god's feet kicked up dirt as he soared toward his wife, hands entangling in her braids and midnight skin within seconds. They held each other as though they could only breathe when the other was around. By that point, many things were beginning to be seen in a clear way. Outside of the labyrinth, there were no guards, only Thor and Sigyn, waiting for the rest of their company to return. Not Ullr, Astrid immediately noticed. Not Ullr and not Darrow.

How long had Freyr been waiting for them? How long had Ivaldi suspected that the Aesir would try to grab at his prized weapon?

The moment they stepped out of the maze, and Astrid's eyes fell upon the prince, it all rang quite simple.

His drunken outburst the day before was all it took. Everything had come to them so simply: the map, Darrow, the way forward. It was far too simple, and not even one of them realized it. Except Loki, Astrid reminded herself. He and Sigyn were the only ones to want to retreat, who asked for it, who begged for it.

Astrid was a fool, just as they had said.

But no longer was she simply a quiet fool, a submissive fool. Her eyes fell upon her Prince, her god, her lover, and there was only one thing she could do.

Thor jogged to her, a relieved smile pulling back at his lips. "Astrid," he murmured. "We heard the maze begin to crumble. I thought—"

Astrid ripped her blade out and angled it toward him. The tip glinted as it pressed against the pulsing in his throat. "Take another step," she whispered, "and I'll gut you right where we stand."

"Astrid," Thor said, his voice louder. Danger swarmed to his crystal eyes. "Stow your blade."

"Why? Because you are my prince? My god? My lover?"

He flicked the steel away as if it were nothing. "Because I have told you to."

"Darrow is dead."

Thor frowned. "A pity."

"His killer," Astrid growled, her anger rising, "dared to utter the same words in my presence."

Sigyn approached slowly, one arm wrapped around the trickster. "Astrid," she said, an unease in her voice. "What has happened?"

"Freyr," she muttered, "met us in the Hall of Victories. He is what beat your husband." She gestured to Loki, whose wound was beginning to close on its own. "He is what stole our skald's life. He took the hammer. How do you suppose he knew of our plans? How do you think Ivaldi knew how to charm his map?"

Astrid raised her blade again, despite it being meaningless against the boulder. She stepped closer still, unfearing, thrusting the blade toward him. "*How* do you suppose, Thor?"

Lightning danced in his eyes, but he remained silent.

"You, my Prince," Astrid whispered. "It is always you, isn't it?"

"Astrid."

"What?" She pressed the flat edge of her sword against her own throat. "Do you wish to strike me next? Rid the world of your loyal shadow? Is that it?"

"Remove that blade."

"Why?" It sliced her skin, but she barely felt the pain. "You'd rather punish me with your own hands, right? You'd rather—"

Thor shot forward as thunder clapped overhead. He slapped the sword from her hands, his hand wrapping around her neck seamlessly. He grabbed her hair by the fistful, keeping her trapped beneath his eyes. "Because," he growled, his nose grazing her own, "you are my snarling wolf, and your anger is precious to me. But the moment you raise your hand to me again, I'll rid the world of its Swordslayer." His grip grew tight, and the air was squeezed out of her. "Do you understand me?"

Swordslayer.

Astrid could only nod, the ability to speak ripped away from her.

When he released her, she fell to her knees, just as he had intended.

"Swordslayer," Sigyn repeated.

Thor was already walking away with his hands clenched tightly at his sides. Lightning sparked on the edges of his blonde curls, smoke trailing up and over his head like a storm cloud. "The fleeing Dwarves," he muttered. "That was what they called her."

Astrid stared at the ground, heaving. Blood trickled from her throat and splashed against the floor. The rage did not leave her. It was all she had, it was all that was left.

Shoving herself to her feet, Astrid gathered her remaining strength and stormed away from the wall. She knew not where she was headed and hardly cared that there were footsteps following her. There just needed to be space. There needed to be something, or she might've imploded and taken them all down with her.When she stopped walking, Astrid slid down against the side of a building. It was a tavern, she assumed, from the reeking scents coming from it and the muffled sounds from within. A courtyard was in front of it, but she lingered in an alleyway's shadow. Dwarves were beginning to leave their homes and prepare for the day, mostly heading toward the mines, unaware of the break-in that had happened hours before.

Silence continued for a moment, until Loki took a seat by her side.

"What of Ullr?" Astrid finally asked.

Loki sighed. "Sigyn says he disappeared when the wall fell between us. This"—he paused to pull something out of his pocket—"was all that was left behind." It was the god's casing of ash, for his rune sorcery, something he was never without.

"Do you think he is dead?"

"No," Loki replied. "Not if the Vanir took him."

"How can you be so sure?"

"It is the way of war, farmer girl. You should get used to it."

Astrid looked away and brought her knees up to her chest. "I am covered in blood," she whispered.

"We can clean it."

"No," she murmured. "It is deeper than that. I am *covered*."

Loki remained quiet as he leaned his head against the side of the wall, his chest rising and falling steadily. After a few minutes, he reached into his pockets and retrieved a silver chain. At the very end of it was a charm, carved from wood. He reached for Astrid's hands, letting the jewelry fall into her palm.

Astrid held the charm up. It was a sword, small and dainty. "What is this?"

"For you."

She eyed him. "I did not take you to be a crafter of jewelry, trickster."

"Perhaps not," he murmured. "But it might protect you."

"From what?"

Loki's eyes grew clouded. "From what I cannot shield you from."

The charm lay delicately against her palm. She ran her fingers over the grooves, the miniscule lines and purposeful chips. Perhaps the thing was quickly done, carved from a duller blade not entirely meant to strike through wood, but it did not change the beauty Astrid saw within it. She tried to imagine when the god even found the time to make it but couldn't come up with an answer. How did she manage to let herself be surprised by them?

"Don't tell me that you won't wear it," Loki teased, his brow already rising in amusement. "Since you are already spoken for."

The heat that rushed to her face was untimely and, most of all, *embarrassing*. Astrid jerked her head away within the same second, ignoring the trickster's musical laugh and how fast she managed to pull it over her head.

It felt heavy, for a moment, before settling against her as if it had always been there. A warmth passed over her, but she tried to shove it away. The magic within the jewelry might have sought to calm the raging anger coursing through her, but Astrid was in no rush to be rid of it. In some ways, it was all she had left.

"I believe I have made the wrong choice," she whispered.

"When?"

"In following Thor."

Loki laughed lightly. "I could have told you that long ago." Sensing the lack of teasing in her voice, the trickster sighed deeply. "You have a lifetime to turn away, Astrid. Perhaps you might seek another homestead."

She scoffed. "Can you *honestly* see me being a farmer?"

"You were one once, weren't you?"

"Once," she whispered, "I was untouched by divinity."

"You can be again."

"How, when I cannot remember what it was my hands did before I met him?"

Loki pressed his lips together, rendered silent.

"You see," Astrid murmured, "there is no other path for me. There is only war, there is only death. I am covered in blood."

He scooted closer, their shoulders touching. It was peaceful, for a moment, but it was all Astrid could take. Anymore, and she might've crumbled as his feet, reduced to a shell of what she once was. No matter what, she needed to keep going. Perhaps, by the end of it all, Astrid might return home to Asgard and feel relieved.

Though that felt far away, now.

Within the courtyard, a town crier's voice chimed through the air. It was burly and low, that of a Dwarf, but still carried to where they were hunkered down. Miners were beginning to pass through the courtyard in groups, and the crier expelled whatever news they needed to hear. Most of it ran over Astrid's head, but there was a small part of it that reached her, striking a nerve deep within her.

"Great and Honorable Ivaldi," the town crier said, "celebrates a union with the Vanir, poised to deliver a great gift that might bless our realm for ages to come. On the 'morrow, we bid our visitor farewell!"

Astrid perked up. "Did you hear that?"

"Freyr will leave tomorrow," Loki murmured. "And take Mjolnir with him."

"Forget the damned hammer." Astrid was already beginning to stand. "It is Ullr that I think of."

Loki rose alongside her, his brow furrowed. "You think the Vanir will take him to Vanaheim with him?"

"You said it yourself. It is the way of war."

The corner of his lip tugged into a smirk. "You may be right. But what is there for us to do?"

"Something stupid, I suppose."

Loki's sharp and musical laugh filled the air as they crept through the shadows, side by side, cloaked by his illusionary magic.

Loki and Astrid burst through the doors of their hideout: the abandoned shack across Storby.

Their other two companions rested quietly within, both on opposite sides of the room. While Sigyn greeted Loki the moment he entered, Astrid was left on her lonesome, merely staring at the prince where he sulked.

"So," Thor drawled after a moment or two, pushing himself off the wall, "my two greatest opposers return."

Astrid swallowed the bile that rose in her throat. If there was anything she knew, it was the boulder's great ability to hold onto grudges. While she wasn't entirely different herself, she could stow it away when the time came. He'd always watch her in a way he did not before, she knew. Suddenly, Astrid was something he needed to fear, if that was at all possible. Maybe not, but a growing unrest needing to be watched.

"Freyr will be leaving with the hammer tomorrow," Astrid said.

Sigyn frowned. "We already knew we'd be returning home without our prize. What of it?"

"Did you all plan on leaving Ullr behind?"

Thor scoffed as he approached. "The god can handle himself."

"In the hands of Freyr," Astrid murmured, "I do not think so."

"Let me guess. You and the *brilliant* trickster have forged a plan capable of outsmarting a Vanir, along with the entire Dwarven realm." Thor loomed over her with his arms crossed over his chest. "Is that right?"

Astrid's hands tightened into fists at her sides. "Jealous, Thor?"

"You—"

"Jealous that we managed to come up with something before you did?"

Thor's hair began to stand up as sparks of lightning rippled up and down his arms. "Tell me," he whispered, growing closer still, "What brilliance have you managed to summon?"

"We might retrieve the hammer still," Astrid said, ignoring how her heart hammered relentlessly against her chest, "and uncover Ullr, but going where Ivaldi might never expect."

"And where might that be?"

"His private estate."

Thor's brow furrowed. "How could we do that?"

"Loki is a master shapeshifter," she explained. "And Sigyn's shadow magic allows her to travel anywhere unseen."

"And you and I?"

Astrid raised her chin. "We might be held in chains if you allow your stubbornness to be quelled for a moment or two."

Thor's laugh shocked her at first, as it echoed through the small shack. He backed away as he shook his head, glancing over his shoulder at the trickster. "You have heard of this plan, trickster?"

Loki nodded. "It is sound."

The prince did not seem satisfied, for reasons Astrid could not understand, but he was rendered silent. Not even a hint of an argument came from his sneer. He merely waved a hand through the air, defeated, and stormed past Astrid, his shoulder making sharp contact against her as he walked by. The door to the shack slammed behind him.

TWELVE

Astrid found Thor upon the shack's rooftop, looking over Storby.

Sometimes, when her guard was down and the world forgotten, Astrid could look upon him and imagine that he was simply a mortal like herself. There was no thorny crown wrapped around his head, no purple cloak hanging down his back. And there, in the dark shadows, Thor looked like a man. A façade of comfort washed over her. The moment he had his crown, he took on an otherworldly look, dangerous and unbeatable. Without it, Thor was simply the boulder, a god with an unprecedented temper. Astrid allowed herself to imagine him as something else entirely, and carefully approached him, trying not to slip on the rusty shingles.

Thor did not move when she took a seat beside him.

"I did not think the bard would die."

Astrid looked over her shoulder at the prince. "I don't believe any of us did."

"Most creatures who travel with gods meet their end in such a way," he murmured and avoided meeting her eyes. "But I did not think it would be his fate."

She tried to swallow the words, but there was a hefty lump in her throat. Never had he made a point to distinguish the line between mortal and divine. He liked to praise her mortality, praise the wrinkles slowly growing along her skin, praise the age that coursed through her long hair. The first time he found a gray strand, a single one, buried within her auburn curls, Thor held it like a prize, like a relic. Astrid assumed that it was his way of respecting the fragile life she lived, but then, she figured it might've been something else.

Maybe the immortal Prince of Asgard eyed mortality in the same way she bowed before his divinity.

Astrid shook the thought away. It was foolish.

Sound flurried overhead. Astrid raised her face to the facade of a sky above them. It was merely stone, she knew, but something was flying across it as though there were stars and a moon. Her eyes narrowed as she stared.

Valkyrie.

It wasn't entirely unusual to see the winged women traveling between realms, but it wasn't impossible. There were no fallen warriors for them to collect, no souls that might've earned an eternity of glory in Odin's Valhalla, awaiting the horns of Ragnarök. Either way, it was a spectacle to see them.

Ever since Astrid was a girl, she had always imagined what it would have been like to be one of Odin's angels. They were limitless in travel, seeing all that there was to see, but always returning home. Their power came from the All-Father himself, so that if he were to ever perish, their ability to fly between realms would go with him.

"Look," she whispered, pointing for Thor to see.

He raised his head and watched as the Valkyrie disappeared in the distance.

"To be a Valkyrie," she murmured. "To fly away. Isn't it tempting?"

"Do you wish to leave?"

Astrid eyed him. "Why does it sound like you want to accuse me of something?"

"Is there something for you to be guilty of?"

"Thor," she groaned, turning away from him. "I came to try and make peace with you, but—"

"I gave you your chance to leave this all behind," he whispered, "or did you forget that?"

Astrid's eyes narrowed. "I do not forget our first meeting, if that is what you are implying."

"I gave you your chance." Thor pulled his legs up to his chest, wrapping his arms around his knees like a child. When the murmur left his lips, Astrid thought she had only imagined it. "*I'll burn your fucking wings.*"

"Sometimes," Astrid snapped, "I believe you are no better than a boy."

Thor laughed, though there was no humor in it. "That is not how you speak to your god."

"Tell me, Prince, what it is you wish for me to regard you as?" Astrid paused to turn and face him fully, her hands wrangling with his own to unwrap him from himself. "Your lover or worshipper?"

"Who is to say I cannot have both?"

"I do."

Thor smirked, his eyes lighting up mischievously. "You should whisper my name like a prayer," he murmured. "As you have in the past."

Her cheeks burned red in embarrassment, though there weren't any eyes around. "Like I said," she grumbled, "you are no better than a *boy*."

He reached for her, pulling her close to his side on the rooftop. "Forgive me," he said against her hair, pressing a short kiss to her scalp. "I am unruly, I know."

"Only unruly?"

"Tell me you hate me, and I might change."

Astrid sighed. "You know I cannot say that," she said. "And you shouldn't need it to change."

"Oh, but I do." Thor held one hand around both her wrists like a shackle. "If you don't, I will be forced to regard you as mine, forevermore."

The desire for him that rested deep within her rose to the surface at the words, despite everything else screaming to be rid of him. He was a disease that spread relentlessly through her veins, and she had no power to stop it. Or, perhaps, she had the cure for it right in front of her and was inherently blind to it.

"How is it that you can go from holding your hand over my throat in one minute," Astrid said, "and whispering in my ear the next?"

Thor laughed again. "It is my specialty."

"I do not think so."

"And you know me, don't you?"

Astrid pulled away slightly, but his grip did not loosen. "I do."

"Sure," he replied sarcastically.

"I know you, Thor," she snapped. "Perhaps you'd prefer to ignore that or act as if there's no one in all the Nine Realms who can truly see you, but it isn't true. *I know you.*"

Thor's irritation simmered, but he did not grow angry, not with her hands fitting so perfectly within one of his own. "Fine," he grumbled. "If you insist on knowing me so well, what do you see?"

She twisted around to face him. "You are afraid."

"Well, *now* you're just having fun."

"I'm being dreadfully serious, Thor."

His eyes sparked with lightning. "There isn't a living soul who would dare to call me afraid."

"It's not like you are killing me, is it?"

For a moment, his hands tightened over her own. "Point taken."

Astrid breathed in deeply, watching the man begin to look like the young Prince she had fallen in love with. But, she reminded herself, he was not just a man. "I make you feel a certain way," she whispered, "And it frightens you."

Thor remained silent as his brow furrowed.

"It is why you acted that way before," she continued. "You are frightened by what binds us together."

"And what would that be?"

"That is a question for the Norn."

Thor chuckled. "I suppose it is."

A silence overtook them upon the rooftop. Astrid tried to remember the fury she felt when leaving the labyrinth but could hardly raise it again. Perhaps Thor did know how death trailed after him, how his reckless and careless actions landed them in hot water, time and time again. Questions hovered over Astrid's head like a storm cloud, forever left unanswered.

Thor leaned toward her, his warm lips testing her own in a single swipe.

In another life, Astrid might not have given in to him.

But it was not another life.

Astrid sank into his kiss instantly. Finally, it no longer felt like the world was catching aflame all around her. She weighed nothing as she fell into it, as he made up for every word that had been spoken between them. She wanted him to kiss away the scars, to press his lips to the cuts against her neck, to use their twisted love as a bandage. All she needed was a hint of it, a small fragment of an undying devotion, but she could not pull away. That was the addiction, she realized, though she wasn't sure if it was to Thor himself or the divinity that coursed beneath his skin.

The kiss was supposed to satisfy her never-ending yearning, but all it did was forge something new. A dangerous desire, not something as simple as hunger, but rather a malicious taunt. She craved more, needed more, would kill for more.

When he pulled away, allowing her to gulp down much-needed air, Thor's hand reached for her neck to hold her in the way he preferred.

The moment his fingers brushed against the nape of her neck, the necklace she wore burned into a fiery light. It snapped out against the prince's touch, as though he reached through a cage to pet a feral dog, only to have the animal's jaws clamp down on his fingers. Thor retracted instantly, lightning already bursting at the seams of his eyes.

"What is this?" he hissed, his gaze glued to the charm hanging from her neck.

Astrid reached for it, but it did not harm her. "I-I—"

"You reek of magic," Thor seethed. "Who gave that to you? Where did you get it?"

Her heart was racing differently. She knew exactly what it was, suddenly, and could not search for a way out of the problem she created. "It was a gift," she replied.

"From *who*?"

She gulped. "Loki, he..."

Thor released her hands, finding his way to the back of her head, collecting her hair by the fistful. He pulled her head back, craning her neck till she could see his livid expression. "Tell me," he hissed, the danger radiating off him, "did the trickster kiss you as I have before wrapping this cursed thing across your neck?"

Astrid gritted her teeth. The truth lay on the tip of her tongue. *No,* she thought. *Of course, he didn't.* Loki was as devoted to his wife as the root was devoted to the earth. What bound them together was something entirely different than that. It was love, she knew, but a love of the soul. A love of a body ripped in half, dropped in two different times.

It was Thor's sudden and raging jealousy that made her want to lie. Loki gave her a protective totem, one that must've been specifically charmed to shield her from Thor's touch. More specifically, it would be his touch around her throat, in the way he did when they had emerged from Ivaldi's labyrinth.

"Do you want the truth, Prince?" Astrid seethed. "Loki has shown me more love and humanity than you ever had. Is that what you wish to hear? That his presence makes me feel seen in ways you'll *never* be capable of? How much does it rile your blood to know that your loyal worshipper would rather kneel before the trickster?"

Thor drew as close as he could without touching her. "Do not make me ask again," he hissed.

"Are you out of your mind?" Astrid shouted, no longer caring that they were on a rooftop. "Of course he didn't! Loki is—"

He crashed down upon her like a tidal wave. His kiss was demanding, violent, authoritative. With another strong fist, Thor ripped the charm off her neck, the chain slicing against her back without warning.

When he pulled away, they were both breathless and wanting, chests heaving with desire.

"Do you think of him?" His voice was low and trembling, not out of fear, but rather a sign that his edge was approaching, and there was little to be done about keeping him back any longer. "As I hold you this way? As I touch you like –"

Astrid jerked beneath his touch, her hands desperately shoving at him. The agonizing ache that burrowed its way into her chest cried for him, wanting to close the gap between their lips and pray for her god's forgiveness. The loyal servant within her, the worshipper she had always been raised to be, wanted to fall to her knees and kiss his feet.

But now, she wished to burn down the temple she built for him, even if it happened to be her own shell of a body.

Astrid wrestled her way out of his touch, sliding backwards on the loose shingles that lined the rooftop. "You are jealous of the trickster," she hissed, not moving even when he stormed forward, even when he tried to grasp her again, even when the chain of the necklace lashed and tore at her frail skin. "You are *jealous*!"

"I am your religion," he growled, taking her by the throat with a single swipe. Thor lifted, effortlessly, and her feet skidded against the ground. Beneath his fingers, her pulse beat to the rhythm of striking lightning. "I am your everything. Why should I be jealous of that which is below me?"

She was not thinking, she was unraveling, she was desperate. Astrid wished to be free, wished to turn the clock back and take the out he once gave her. She spit hatefully against his cheek. "He is more than anything you'll ever be."

His crystal-colored eyes went staggeringly wide. The rageful demeanor he once carried cracked and splintered, revealing the broken man beneath. Thor flinched against her words, his hand loosening from around her throat before releasing entirely. His eyes lowered, gravitating back to the necklace dangling from his fingers. Scarlet blood stained patches of it.

As his head rose, slow and menacing, the amulet rose alongside it, before it was directly in front of Astrid's face. "Watch me rip the head off your beloved protector."

Her eyes went wide. "Thor!"

But he was already moving.

Thor scaled down the side of the shack without a moment to lose, the sound of his fists crashing through the door echoing throughout Storby.

Astrid rushed after him, already hearing the strained noises coming from Loki and the disgruntled fighting from Sigyn. She burst through the front door to see Thor on top of the trickster god, his wide and burly hands wrapped around Loki's throat. Beneath him, Loki thrashed and croaked, scratching and desperately clawing at the boulder's face.

Behind them, Sigyn's hands glowed a mystical grey, her magic rising to the surface.

Running forward, Astrid's arms wrapped around Thor's neck within an instant, her strength feeling minuscule and empty against his own. But all she could think about was losing another one close to her heart. How could she live any longer if Loki was ripped away from her, the man she did not even have? The man she would never claim as her own?

Astrid snatched the amulet from the ground and pressed the charm against the side of Thor's face. A blinding white light erupted through the shack as he flung himself backward, desperately shoving her off around his neck.

Astrid skidded as she hit the floor, the charm cracking in two within her palm.

Thor breathed heavily, like a madman, as he pointed an accusatory finger down at Loki. "Usurper," he whispered. "Always eager to take that which belongs to me."

Loki stared up at him with wild eyes.

"The moment we set foot back in Asgard," he seethed, "you will be *gone*."

"You cannot—"

"You will be *gone!*" Thor's voice boomed through the shack. "Let me see you once more beside my mortal, and I'll serve your head to Sigyn on a silver platter!"

Thor stormed off, curving around and retreating to the secluded hallway within the shack. And, as if there were shackles around her wrist pulling her along behind him, Astrid rose to her feet and weakly followed, ignoring the feeling of Loki's stare burning into the side of her head. All the while, a phrase repeated in the back of her mind, sounding more like a death sentence than something loving, something adoring.

My mortal.

THIRTEEN

Astrid staggered forward as the Dwarf yanked on the chains.

Beside her, Thor's wrists were shackled in the same fashion, binding them together through iron and steel. She eyed him for what felt like the millionth time that day, just waiting for the moment when he would snap and change. After the events of the night before, Astrid never thought he'd agree to be chained and led through the city for their plan. But he never once put up a fight, simply remained quiet and stuck his hands out for the shackles. Perhaps it was the deadly glimmer in his eyes that caught her attention, as if he had another reason for agreeing, one that the rest of the company was not aware of.

The Dwarf leading them toward Ivaldi's mansion was squat and burly, with a hefty helm upon his head and a long, braided beard falling so low it reached the top of his feet. The Dwarf held the chains in one hand and an axe in the other, jerking them forward harshly with every step he took.

The Dwarf angled his head over his shoulder slightly, his eyes flashing a sharp purple before fading into something brown and warm.

Loki.

Everything, so far, was going according to plan.

Within Ivaldi's mansion, the Vanir envoy would gather to collect Mjolnir and retreat to Vanaheim, their home realm. The Dwarves, in return, were presented with a hefty sum for the price of their exchange. And, Astrid hoped, amid it all, Ullr was somewhere, just waiting for the company to turn up. As long as he was still alive, Astrid had a kindling of hope within her chest.

Before they left for their final mission, and after the fight between the gods, Astrid managed to have a second alone with Loki. The guilt lived within her so easily, and even more so then. He faced the boulder's wrath for taking pity upon her, and Astrid was nearing the point where she could no longer live with herself.

"Usurper," was the first thing Loki murmured when she stood beside him in front of the abandoned shack.

She looked up at him. "What?"

"Did you hear what he had called me?" He shook his head and said it again. "Usurper."

"I'm—"

"Do you know how long I have served the Bleeding Throne of Asgard?"

Just hearing the name of the holy and revered seat in which the All-Father sits sent a chill down Astrid's spine. But, instead of forcing out the apology she was trying to muster, she simply shook her head.

"I knew Odin when he was simply a fledgling," Loki murmured. "When he and his brothers struck the vein in Ymir to render him dead. When he carved Midgard out from the beast's stomach." He shook his head. "Usurper."

Astrid watched him with wide eyes. "There is little I know about where you come from."

"And that is how it will remain."

"Why?"

Loki faced her, and a despair she could not pinpoint began to fester within his dark gaze. "Because it is not suitable for your ears," he said. "And I do not wish to plague you with knowledge you are incapable of holding."

Gulping down her fear, Astrid reached for his hand like a lost child. Her fingers curled around his own. For the first time in a long time, the first thing Astrid felt was not the god's divinity sinking into her soul. But, instead, there was only warmth. A comfort that she was not worthy of.

Loki's fingers tightened. "I was once quite envious of you, farmer girl."

"Me?"

He nodded. "But now," he paused, a slight tremble in his head. When he met her gaze, his indescribable age was apparent, for just a split second. "Now I only fear for you."

And before she had the chance to tell him how sorry she truly was, Loki's hand loosened around her own, and he walked away.

Astrid was pulled out of her reverie as they climbed the stairs leading up to Ivaldi's private mansion. When they had first ventured into the estate, Astrid had only seen it from afar or from above. The house itself was the grandest thing within the entire realm. Most of the Dwarves seemed to live in some sense of poverty, always needing another run through the mines to afford their family's next meal. Ivaldi, however, must have been rolling in exuberant amounts of gold to manage something like that.

Pillars decorated the front of the mansion. Gates and fences with prickly, sharp tips surrounded the entire estate. The mansion itself was a few stories high, with wide windows that spanned from the very floor to the roof's tip on every side. Statues carved from marble or porcelain were positioned like guards upon the manor's corners, each representing a different Dwarf from legend. Astrid, upon further glance, believed them all to have been the fabled creatures said to hold up the four ends of the earth.

As they came to the front doors, Astrid caught a glimpse of movement through the shadows, Sigyn's sterling white eyes meeting her own. Guards met them at the doors, talking in the Dwarven language to Loki before mumbling in agreement and letting him through. Astrid did her best not to look around in wonderment but could hardly help herself. The architecture and priceless artifacts that Ivaldi kept throughout his entire estate were nothing to scoff at.

Guards dressed in silver armor led Loki through the halls till they came upon a set of wide double doors. Loki jerked on the chains a few times as he followed the guards, earning a few curses from Thor under his breath. Astrid glanced at him as they waited for the doors to be opened.

Being successful meant retrieving both Ullr and the hammer, but it all rode on one thing.

Thor's temper.

If the prince kept his head on straight, Astrid was sure that the day would end in triumph. The Vanir would be empty-handed, and they would be riding the rainbow bridge back home in a matter of minutes. Astrid kept repeating the thought in the back of her mind as they drew nearer to Ivaldi.

The room in which the doors opened was that of a throne room, much to Astrid's surprise. As far as she was concerned, there was no single ruler over Svartalfheim. Some governors overlooked the mining towns, but Ivaldi was no politician. He was simply a master blacksmith, a curator of deadly creations that managed to sway even the gods in his favor. Somehow, that single notion managed to get Ivaldi an ornate throne to sit upon.

"A glorious day, indeed!"

Ivaldi rose from his purple, velvety throne. He dressed in long robes, ones that dragged behind his feet when he walked. Beneath his robes, a delicate sheen of armor glimmered beneath the chandelier overhead. He was quite a handsome Dwarf, Astrid realized, but not in the same way that she considered Darrow to be handsome. The difference was that Ivaldi carried his crassness proudly, like a badge, a sneer upon his curved lips.

Guards remained on every side of him as he approached Loki, who still looked like nothing more than a dutiful mining Dwarf.

"You have managed quite the feat," Ivaldi said as he clapped his hairy hand upon Loki's shoulder. "Capturing both the Aesir god of thunder and..." Ivaldi peered over his shoulder toward his guards. "What is it they call her?" There were a few mumbles before he laughed sharply. "Right, right. The Swordslayer."

Astrid's lips poked up slightly, hardly able to help herself.

"Well, this is *quite* the busy day around here," Ivaldi continued, "So won't we pay this good servant, and bring the prisoners to the dungeons below?"

Behind Ivaldi, one of the guards tossed a pouch in the air and caught it with the same hand, coins jingling within.

Astrid glanced toward Thor, whose head was angled down, his piercing stare holding onto Ivaldi intensely.

The guard placed the pouch within Loki's hands and stepped toward the chains behind him, the shackles that bound Astrid and Thor together. As Loki pulled open the pouch, playing the part of a greedy Dwarf, an inky black darkness burst out from it and swallowed him whole. Astrid's eyes went wide, stopping the shout in the back of her throat before she gave away his cover.

He is a god, she told herself. *He can handle himself.*

But as the smoke began to clear, Ivaldi, making a *tsk* noise with his teeth as he circled them, the Dwarf was no longer there. Loki stood in his place, the magic shifting him into the creature, disappearing. He looked at his hands in bewilderment before looking back toward Ivaldi.

"How did you—"

"Do you all take me for a fool?" Ivaldi stood in front of them, at the steps that led up to his throne. "Well, perhaps I *am* a fool, but did you take me to be a fool with no friends in high places?"

Loki's hand twitched, and the chains began to burn and sizzle away, till there were no shackles around Astrid or Thor's wrists.

Ivaldi laughed. "You Aesir," he muttered before spitting on the ground beside their feet. "I would tell you to give Odin my regards, but...well, you won't be leaving Svartalfheim, will you?"

The Dwarf's shrill laughter echoed as his guards pulled out their axes and began to form a tight circle around the trio.

Thor growled, the lightning sparking around his wrists. "Trickster," he snarled. "Our weapons."

Loki's whispers filled the air as his magenta colored magic curled all around them. Once it reached Astrid's hands, it took shape into her familiar blade, resting within her hands like an extension of her arm. Beside her, the magic manifested into a spear in Thor's hands. He twirled it around menacingly, thunder cracking right outside the windows.

Thor released an echoing roar. "*Fight*!"

Astrid shot forward like a snake, her viper hand slashing and swiping through the Dwarvish armor. She curved in and out of the crowd as if she were a dancer, the music only coursing through her ears.

Sigyn's *skyggemagi* hummed as she stepped out from the shadows, materializing within the midst of battle. Sharp whips trailed down her limbs and sliced through the air as she whipped them around, loud whistles following every strike. The Dwarven armor shuddered against the magic.

The whip snapped around the wrist of one of the Dwarf's, but the creature caught it with his other hand, wrestling the magic bravely. Sigyn yanked and growled as her power grew, entirely unaware of the second Dwarf beginning to creep up behind her.

Astrid's blade sunk deep through sterling armor and she ripped it out; her eyes stuck on the Dwarf that was slowly trailing up to Sigyn with a glimmering blade in hand. Astrid pulled her hand sharply behind her head and flung it forward, watching the stained dagger twirl through the air. It plunged down into the center of the Dwarf's chest, and his weapon clattered to the floor, catching Sigyn's attention.

The sorceress looked over her shoulder. "Good aim," she said, her lip turning up. "For a farmgirl."

Astrid laughed, forgetting herself, and jogged to retrieve her sword. She only managed a step when more Dwarven guards barreled into the room, one letting their shoulder slam into her chest as they approached. Astrid staggered back and skidded, her back landing sharply against a pillar. The Dwarf ran toward her, a garish battle cry filling the air as he raised a double-bladed axe over his armored head.

Humanity grasped at her, and she was petrified, stuck in place without a weapon to protect her. The Dwarf loomed, his blade releasing a shrieking noise as it ripped through the air.

Clang!

Astrid's eyes snapped open to see a tall figure standing in front of her, long dark hair tickling her nose.

Loki.

The trickster clenched his teeth as he braced his staff, Laevateinn, against the Dwarf's steel axe. He shoved the Dwarf back and threw a smirk over his shoulder at Astrid. "Having fun yet, farmer girl?"

"Oh," she mouthed, grasping a handle upon his belt and unsheathing a short sword, "*loads.*"

Charging forward side-by-side, Astrid dove into the remaining battle with a newfound burst of energy. For a split second, as iron clashed upon iron, she forgot about where she was. She merely fought beside her closest companions, the people she could never imagine not being in her life. Even if she knew it was going to end soon, she only held onto it as tightly as she could, desperate to know what it felt like to truly be free.

The chaos simmered down as the ground around them was littered with the bodies of fallen Dwarves. In the distance, horns bellowed and erupted.

"Reinforcements," Loki murmured as he heard them. "We must continue before they arrive."

Astrid sheathed her sword, already nodding. "We should go to the dungeons."

Sigyn materialized at her right, one brow raised. "For what reason, farmer girl?"

"The only one here capable of killing Aesir gods is the Vanir himself," she replied. "Ivaldi mentioned dungeons. I can only assume that is where Freyr is, along with the hammer and Ullr."

Thor, who took up an axe from one of the fallen, shook his head, low and slow. "The Dwarf needs to be dealt with."

"The Dwarf has summoned an army to come and defend him," Astrid argued, pointing toward the doors, where the horns grew louder. "They are far more than what we can handle."

He glanced at her over his shoulder, eyes sparking with lightning. "For *you*."

"Thor," she snapped, rushing to stand in front of him. "Listen to yourself. The All-Father sent us here for the hammer!"

"It will come to me."

Behind them, Loki scoffed.

Astrid shook her head. "How can you be like this? What about Ullr, then?"

"Ullr," Thor murmured, his eyes not meeting her own, "knew what he was getting himself into long ago, even if it meant his death."

Her eyes went wide as she staggered backwards, feeling as though she had been struck through the chest with a blade. "Thor, this is not you. This does not *have* to be you!"

When he finally met her gaze, there was a dark heaviness within them that Astrid did not wish to even spend a second trying to understand. "For someone who claims to know me," he whispered, "you know very little."

Astrid's despair was beginning to mount to new heights, ones that she was unsure that she'd be able to climb back out of. Stepping further away from him, she swallowed the tears that threatened to fall down her cheeks and stormed back toward Loki and Sigyn.

"We will uncover Mjolnir and Ullr," Astrid shouted, "*my Prince.*"

And as she stormed off, gods on either side of her, Astrid wished to have been one herself, to rip the thunder god's throat out with nothing but her bare teeth.

FOURTEEN

Once, long ago, Astrid hated the gods.

She was still a child, nowhere near the time of becoming a soldier in the Royal Guard, and not yet burdened with a massacre she could not even begin to imagine. They were the days when her father would travel through Asgard as a merchant, collecting and selling as he went. Her mother remained at the homestead, tending to the farm and her children. Once a great Vikingr, her mother's old armor and shield hung from the wall like an aged relic. Astrid used to look upon them as though they had been touched by the divine themselves, believing herself to never be worthy to wear such things.

There was a time when she had been plagued with nightmares. They kept her up each night, from when the moon sat at his highest point, till he had fallen beyond the horizon, and the beautiful sun took her turn within the sky. Astrid rocked herself in bed, paced back and forth without disturbing her slumbering sister, and even drank the tea her mother kept under lock and key, all to have a peaceful night.

But it never came.

She dreamt of Ragnarök, she believed, but it was not a vision of the Nine Realms' end time, but perhaps her *own*. Astrid cried at her mother's bosom one late evening, the ravens cawing sharply outside the window.

"Tell me," her mother had cooed, "what is it that you see?"

"A raven before me," Astrid remembered, her eyes falling shut as the images came flooding back to her. "Scratching at my face till everything hurt. And there would be a tree, the branches long like fingers, creaking so loud." She pressed her hands against her ears. "So loud."

Her mother pulled her hands away to kiss her palms. "And then?"

"Three women dressed in golden robes with antlers and empty faces hold a tightly wound thread in their hands," she whispered. "It was shimmering, like it had been pulled out of a star, until they sliced it in half. And the moment it did, the moment it broke apart, I felt as though my insides were aflame."

"And then what happened?"

"They put the thread back together. And I wake up."

For hours, Astrid's mother rubbed her hand along her back, singing quiet lullabies into her ear. It wasn't until it was the early morning, the sun peeking over the horizon, that she finally spoke.

"The Norn have presented your fate onto you," she murmured.

Astrid looked up at her with a puzzled expression.

"Fate weavers," she had said. "You have been claimed."

"Claimed? By whom?"

And the look on her mother's face was something haunting, something incredibly fearful.

"The gods."

Astrid stepped down from the final stair that led into Ivaldi's dungeons with her sword in hand, ready to slay a god.

The dungeon was a singular, narrow hallway that had cages erected on either side of it. At the very end, the hall rounded out into a wide room, with a tall column in the middle connecting it to the ceiling. The cages, as they passed by, were empty and collecting dust.

"Very good, farmer girl," Sigyn murmured from the rear. "Not a single sign of—"

Astrid whipped around, her blade already extended. The time for teasing and jokes was long gone. Now, she was determined, fueled with a rageful passion she was in no hurry to ignore. Suddenly, she needed to prove herself. Not just to her companions, but to the Norn who watched, to the One-Eyed god they needed to return to, to her dead and gone mother.

"Hold your tongue," she whispered.

Sigyn's eyes were wide, but not fearful.

It was Loki who neared her, one hand resting upon the hilt of her blade. "Save your anger for Freyr," he said. "Astrid."

She avoided meeting his gaze, for the trickster god managed to unravel her with the slightest bat of an eye.

Astrid lowered her blade. "I'm—"

"*Hello?*" a familiar voice echoed through the hall. "Oi! I haven' had so much as a *lick* of something to drink since I was thrown in this cesspool! One of you's better be—"

"Ullr!" Astrid shouted, already running.

Near the end of the hall, at one of the final cells, Ullr sat slumped in the corner. Rags fell off his shoulders and waist, exposing his porcelain colored skin and leftover, ashy runes. Sandy-colored hair fell across his face haphazardly as he stood up, rushing toward the bars holding him back.

"Bloody well done, love," Ullr cooed when his eyes landed on her, a lazy smile tugging at his lip. "Took you all long enough!"

Loki stepped forward and went to work on the lock, his fingers laced with his purple magic. "Don't get your panties in a wad," he muttered.

Ullr laughed, short and loud. "Dear me, trickster. Have you missed me?"

Though Astrid did not want to pull her gaze away from their lost friend, there was an echoing in the back of her mind that tempted her. She looked over her shoulder, into the wide and round room at the back of the dungeon. A figure stepped out from behind the column, dressed in shocking golden armor with darkened antlers across the breastplate.

The breath hitched in her throat.

Freyr.

In one hand, his shimmering sword glinted against the fragile torchlight. In the other, the prize they had been searching for echoed an immense power. A boxy hammer with a leather-wrapped handle, runes carved into the corners. It was colored ebony, but staring at it for too long made her eyes sting.

Mjolnir.

Suddenly, she realized, Astrid was surrounded by gods. For a moment, she felt like collapsing, but that was simply ludicrous. She basked within it, instantly, soaking in the rays of gold and feeling it stream through her blood. Perhaps it wasn't the strongest way to reach it, but she hardly cared. A simple mortal, an Asgardian, mingling with the immortal creatures as if she were one of them. She felt the urge to tear into her own flesh, to see what lay beneath, to prove herself wrong.

But it was as intoxicating as Sigyn made it out to be.

Astrid brought her blade forth and approached the Vanir god. She felt like iron.

"Oi!" Ullr's voice echoed out behind her. "Spitfire! Where are you—"

"*Astrid*!" Loki was coming, his fingertips just grazing her arm. "Astrid!"

Desperate and fleeting.

Astrid stepped over the threshold as the world shifted around her.

The moment she entered the round room, the mechanics within the walls moved, and the metal door shuddered as it landed on the threshold. In front of her, Freyr moved along the sides of the room with a lowered head—a wolf herding the lamb.

"Peculiar," Freyr murmured. His voice was oddly soothing, despite the circumstances.

Astrid twirled her blade around within her hand, stretching before the battle began.

"You are mortal."

"Does that frighten you?"

Freyr tilted his head. "Interesting," he said. "I do not fear a simple girl. A..." His eyes began to glow as though he captured the sun's rays within them. "Girl descended from *krigers,* I see. I wonder: how did you end up in the throngs of the Aesir?"

"Can't you see it with your seer eyes?"

The light in them faded. "You know little for someone who carries such a strong confidence."

She stopped circling, and he mimicked. "I came in here to slay a Vanir," she called out. "Or would you rather try to bore each other to death?"

Freyr brandished his weapons, the hammer giving off a frightfully powerful energy, one that almost made her stumble. "I see the thread the Norn hold above your head," he said. "It is severed, as though you are meant to die." His eyes flashed something dark. "Or failed to do so once before."

Instantly, Astrid succumbed to her memories, brought back to her old nightmares that her mother claimed to have been messages from the fate weavers. It threatened to pull a shudder out of her, even a nick of fear.

Astrid sliced her blade over her face, the point aimed at his chest. "No longer shall I let a god weaponize my fate," she proclaimed. "I am the crafter of my own fate. I spin the thread, god."

His lip turned up into a smile, stretching till it beamed from ear to ear. "Swordslayer," he said. "It will be an honor to slay you."

Astrid released a shrieking scream, the chant of her family name once expelled before marching into battle, falling from her lips without even a thought to consider it:

"To Valhalla, Skol!"

The world became a haze as she shot across the room toward Freyr. He raised his blade the moment she approached, the iron snapping together with a resounding shock through the air. The force pushed Astrid back a few feet, but she was relentless. There was no future in which she failed again. Mortal or not, Astrid was far more than any of them made her out to be, and she was ready to show it.

The battle sounded like a thunderclap with each strike. Freyr was sharp and stoic, like a statue, simply snapping toward her. Astrid remembered the *Asketre*, the pale cursed tree, and the bow smashed against the side of her face. Even then, years later, the scarring along her sensitive skin tingled. What was it that her father had said?

While everyone else cowers at the cursed wood, we overcome our fear.

Overcome our fear.

Astrid fought like the mortals that made her—strong, heavy-handed, brutal and harsh. She was the cold in the wind, she was the bark of the oldest tree. She was the legend surrounding a cursed wood, she was the weaver of her own fate. Astrid carried the Vikings with her, the Asgardians, the simple guards who loitered over the gods they worshiped.

Ducking beneath his striking arm, Astrid slashed her blade along his uncovered hand, which held onto Mjolnir. The god released a surprised grunt, fingers flexing as the hammer fell from his grasp.

Astrid reached and caught Mjolnir before it had the chance to hit the ground.

Kriger, a voice echoed in the back of her head. *Wield the hammer. Face your foe.*

You are strong.

The ebony weapon suddenly did not weigh a single thing within her palm. She raised it, the power sinking into her skin and fueling her racing blood. It was otherworldly and deadly, something a mortal was never meant to hold.

"You..." Freyr breathed, watching with widening eyes. "You can carry it."

"Why wouldn't I?"

"You are weak," he whispered. "I saw you. You are weak."

Astrid pointed the blunt end of it at the god. "Call me weak another time, and I'll knock your head right off your shoulders."

Anger, finally, burned through the god's calm exterior. He released a grunt before surging forward, brandishing his sword with both hands, tight around the handle. No longer did he move with stunted strikes. He flowed like a rushing lake, smooth and striking.

Astrid met his thrusts with Mjolnir, each strike pushing her further backwards.

Freyr shouted as he whipped around and slammed his elbow into the center of Astrid's chest. The wind left her throat as she was flung toward the wall, her back clapping against it with a resounding *thud.* The floor shook beneath her feet as she landed, only her grip around Mjolnir remaining at the forefront of her mind. Spitting blood onto the floor, she staggered to her feet, ignoring the pulsing pain that began to fester in her side.

"Is that...Is that all you can do?" she croaked, arms raised.

Freyr's bellow was so deep that it made the stone above their heads tremble. Pieces of the ceiling clattered to the floor, a few falling against Astrid's shoulders, but failing to deter her.

They ran forward at the same time, meeting in the middle with a shriek of his greatsword clashing against the hammer's face. Mjolnir echoed as it slammed repeatedly against the Vanir's armor. Instantly, Astrid realized the hammer was far more powerful than anything Freyr had. His sword was rendered useless in the face of it.

Astrid hammered into his armor, watching the gold crease and bend. Perhaps Freyr could not feel the pain, but he grew redder in the face with every hit, the growls echoing out of the back of his throat.

"*Forbann navnet ditt*[1] *!*" Freyr's eyes were wicked and lit up with fury. "You will die, Astrid of Herjan! You will die, and there will be no god to save you then! Nothing but you, and your *mortality*!"

A brilliant light burst around Freyr's figure as the walls of the dungeon started to crumble. He disappeared within a second, fading into the light as if he hadn't been there in the first place. Astrid stared at where he once was with a throbbing heart. She had...won. She had won. The hammer grew heavy in her hands, but she could hardly care. The god retreated, sulking away after delivering a final threat that rang vaguely in her ears.

Astrid's gaze searched for her companions through the door, but there was something fearful in their expressions. Loki's shouts echoed all around her, but she was too far in a haze to make them out. He held the bars and shook like a madman, jerking back when they didn't move to his touch. Beside him, Ullr and Sigyn flared their magic.

But...she had won.

The pride overtook her face as the walls continued falling. How could she care?

Astrid defeated the god.

She began to go toward the door, to try and release it from her side, but was brought to a halting stop.

Astrid choked as something crawled up her throat. She reached for her neck, Mjolnir falling from her grasp and slamming upon

---

1. Translation: Curse your name.

the ground. The sensation continued till she was heaving and collapsing to her knees. Blood spurted from between her lips, trailing down her chin and staining her armor.

I cannot breathe, she screamed. *I cannot...I cannot—*

Her chest caved in before flexing outward. *What is happening?*

Something was wrong, deep inside of her, something she could not see. Astrid fell to her side, the blood pouring onto the floor as spots decorated her vision. The pain at her side erupted as she rolled over.

I cannot breathe.

I cannot—

Sigyn loomed over her. "By the ash tree," her whisper sounded like a scream in Astrid's ears, "*Heal her.*"

Hands pressed in on the sides of her face. A cooling sensation sank into her skin and coursed through her veins. The world grew bright around her, fading into a culmination of noises and footsteps. She could have sworn, within it all, she could see her home.

Herjan, with its bordering mountains and a river striking down the middle. Horses were drinking at the shore. Children were crossing the bridge and chasing each other through the hills. A golden castle sitting between the mountains, so far away, it was simply a dream. And her family homestead, the goats chittering on one side, with the cattle grazing in the east. Her father rode in on his brilliant steed, a warm smile on his face.

"Welcome home, *mitt hjerte,*" he said.

Astrid exhaled sharply before sucking in a gulp of air. She pressed a hand to her chest, feeling the blood damp upon her armor. The pain had gone from her side, the blood no longer clogging her throat and choking her from the inside out. She reached for her face and touched Sigyn's hand, which still rested upon her cheek.

She looked at the sorceress. "I believe I saw Valhalla," she whispered.

Tears were clouding Sigyn's eyes. "Did you?"

"Is it supposed to be like home?"

"Yes, farmer girl. Like coming home."

Astrid cried, unable to stop herself. "I believe I saw Valhalla," she said again.

Suddenly, much to her surprise, Sigyn's arms wrapped around Astrid's shoulders. She squeezed her against her chest, hands gripping her skin like claws.

"How do you forget that you are mortal?" Sigyn whispered, her voice trembling. "How can a creature so small, so frail, forget what they are? Can't you see?"

Astrid let her arms fall around the sorceress. "I see it every day," she murmured. "I am sorry."

"You can take care of yourself," Sigyn said in her ear.

"I know."

"You always will. But we are here now. We will protect you, too."

And Astrid shattered into a million pieces, coming undone in the sorceress's long arms.

FIFTEEN

Astrid carried the hammer through Ivaldi's mansion.

There was a silence that echoed throughout the entire estate as the party of four slowly crept down the halls. No guards lurked around the corner, no Vanir gods or soldiers. No Dwarves waited for them at the end of the line. It was simply still, and it drove an even greater fear into Astrid's weakened heart. The magic Sigyn used to heal her mortal injuries lingered in her eyes, making her foggy and displaced. But there was no time to slow down or even take a breath.

Somehow, the strength of Mjolnir seemed to seep into her own. The longer she held onto it, the more like a corpse she felt. It weighed upon her arm like an entire body, pulling her closer and closer to the ground. Astrid carried it, still, despite the pain it brought. She needed to hold it in front of the thunder god; she needed him to see what it was that his shadow was capable of doing without his hold.

Thor wanted nothing to do with their lost companion or even the weapon they had come for. Instead, he craved more blood upon his steel-tipped spear. He had something to prove, though Astrid was unsure of what that even was. A part of her wished to leave him in the Dwarven realm, let him succumb to his maddening rage, and see to it that another takes the Bleeding Throne after the All-Father. Not him. Not with his deadly stare and lightning-covered fingertips.

Astrid staggered as they went around a corner, slowly nearing the throne room, where they had left Thor.

Loki came to her side at once, an arm tucked beneath her own, the one that gripped onto the hammer still. He raised it. "Deep breaths, my friend. You can carry it. You can."

The words carried her forward as she held Mjolnir up once more. She gave him a firm nod before continuing, her march matching the hammering within her heart. They needed to get the prince and leave the cursed realm before another Vanir decides to take what they believe to be theirs, before the Dwarves retaliate in a way the gods won't be able to handle.

Ullr approached the shut doors to the throne room, snatching up a blade along the way. He used his shoulder to nudge it open, peering through with a cautious eye. He froze halfway, his eyes widening.

"What is it?" Sigyn asked from behind him. "Ullr, what—"

He pushed the door.

Astrid had seen many things in her lifetime. Many things that she wished to forget, others that she held close to her heart. Tragic and beautiful things. But that...that was unlike anything she ever knew. And yet, no matter how horrific it happened to be, Astrid could not pull her eyes away, or even stop her feet from leading her forward, and passing over the threshold of death.

Once, when they first entered the throne room, it was spotless and white. The only color lay within Ivaldi's purple seat, raised a few steps above the rest of the room.

But now, the room was painted red. The reinforcements arrived while Astrid and her companions were down in the dungeons. Every last one of them had been slaughtered, their bodies left around the room in piling heaps. Blood trickled in the cracks in the tile below their feet, slowly crawling around them like an ancient spell. Severed limbs, heads, fingers, they were everywhere.

Thor stood in front of the throne. On the last step, kneeling in front of him, was Ivaldi. The Dwarf's rich attire was stained red and black. It had been torn and shredded in some places, left in pieces around the room. The long, braided beard he carried was shaved down to a whisper along his chin, cuts lining his jaw and neck.

Somehow, she was still surprised.

Even when his entire soul had been soaked in the blood of the innocent, her mind said one thing only: *Something must have happened for him to have done this.*

Something. Anything.

Please.

The moment Astrid stepped over the threshold, Thor looked down at Ivaldi with a widening smile.

He dragged a blade along the Dwarf's neck.

"*No!*" Astrid stepped forward, almost falling over a row of bodies. The hammer dragged her down still, and she staggered, catching herself in the middle of the room.

Thor's eyes were glued to her. "My shadow," he murmured. The prince glided forward, stepping over the countless victims that lay at his feet. He noticed Mjolnir and grinned, the pride unavoidable in his gaze. He reached, his fingers lacing around her own along the hammer's handle. Effortlessly, without even uttering a single word, he slipped the weapon into his hand, pulling it away from Astrid.

"Just like I told you," he said. "It will come to me."

And Thor passed her by, like he had done many times before.

SIXTEEN

Astrid wrote within Darrow's notebook:

"Long ago, in a land of iron and greed,
A Warrior traveling with her Divine,
Fell upon the legend of a mystical hammer."

She shook her head, scribbling out the words for a third time. Doodles of runes scored the margins, Darrow's own handwriting lining the page before the one she worked on. His words were those of sorrow and beauty, the true talent of a skald. And his signature, broad and confident, scored the lines beneath it, forever imprinted upon the page. Astrid focused upon it once more, letting her fingers run across the letters.

A gentle draft rolled by her. Astrid raised her head and looked over the bustling town of Storby. The spot on the rooftop of their abandoned shack proved to be the best spot to see all that there was. Before they left the realm and returned to Asgard, she wished to write a tale in honor of Darrow, to give him the wish he had asked for, but found herself grasping at straws. Unlike the Dwarf, Astrid had little to no talent when it came to writing, or poetry for that matter. Even her voice, used to sing their ancestral songs during harvest time, was compared to Odin's loyal ravens. Which wasn't a compliment, despite her wishing it to be so.

Astrid snapped the book shut and held it tightly against her chest. Thinking that the Dwarf's soul remained within it soothed her, in a way, though it was a sorrowful thought. Where did Dwarves go when they perished? Was there a place such as Valhalla for them? Astrid knew not their ancient fables, or what it was that they believed, but said a short prayer to the wind that Darrow's soul found its way to her ancestor's legendary halls.

"Sigyn has found the tree."

Astrid looked over her shoulder to see the prince. Her stomach swirled, though it wasn't like it used to be. There was a sickening sensation beginning to crawl beneath her skin whenever she looked upon him. As though she knew something was coming, as though she wanted to hide in his arms but cut them off at the same time. She knew not what any of it meant, and it worried her more than the feeling itself.

"Good," she finally said after a prolonged silence. "We leave for home soon."

Thor nodded, slow and stiff. "Astrid."

She could not look at him, no matter how much she tried.

"Why do I feel like everything has changed?"

"Do you wish for it to?"

"No," he whispered, the rooftop creaking as he approached her. "I don't know."

Astrid swallowed as he crouched beside her. "I do not believe much has changed," she said. "Only that I have become what it is you have forged me to be."

Thor shook his head as he reached for her hands, though he hesitated. "I only want you to be what you are," he murmured.

"I am the creature you have made." Astrid finally looked at him, noticing the rain showers in his eyes. "I am what you have shaped me to be."

"What would that be, then?"

Astrid's smile was sad, down in the depths of despair. "Monsters only breed monsters, my love."

The prince's shoulders shuddered. He was curling into a ball, his head falling into her lap with a quiet sigh. He cried, but she did not look upon his face, feeling his shame against her skin. Instead, Astrid wrapped her arms around him as much as she could, determined to keep his pieces together, to keep him from shattering.

And suddenly, the wolf fell asleep against the lamb's wool.

For the first time, Astrid felt at ease when slipping through Sigyn's portal.

In the back of her mind, she still remembered the glimpse into Valhalla she had back at Ivaldi's mansion. It haunted her, though she didn't quite mind. It was everything she left behind, everything she still grasped when her eyes closed. She would see it again, she knew. And her father would coo in her ear, holding her in his arms, just sleeping. It was on the horizon, she told herself. It had to be.

The company was quiet on the journey back to the golden city. Sigyn's portal brought them to the rainbow bridge, where an echoing chasm of darkness tempted them from beneath. Horses waited for them patiently, a few stewards holding them still till they managed to climb on top.

Thor remained at the head of the party with a storm cloud gathering above his head. There wasn't much the prince said since their time on the rooftop, but Astrid wasn't expecting anything for a while. Soon, she imagined, he would beckon her from her duties in the Royal Guard with a dainty flower, whisking her off to some field buried within the mountains to make love beneath the sun. What happened in the land of Dwarves would be a distant memory to the god, something he might remember in passing.

Astrid, as he might press kisses to her neck, would never forget it.

Like the loyal companion he always was, Ullr remained alongside Thor at the front of the pack. They rode beside each other in silence, but perhaps that was the best for both of them. Astrid loitered near the back, not entirely eager to share any words herself. So much rested upon her chest, so much that she could hardly understand.

"You look troubled, my farmer girl."

Astrid allowed herself to smile. "Aren't I always, Loki?"

"I suppose so," he murmured as his steed trotted up alongside her. "How are you?"

She sighed. "I am tired."

"That is all?"

Astrid smirked, holding back her laugh. "Being around you lot makes me feel as though there is a gaping hole in the center of me," she said. "Something that has always been empty, but I never quite noticed it, not until now, at least."

"Well," Loki drawled with a raised brow, "I should've expected something like that."

Astrid laughed, but it sounded hollow.

"There is something I wish to tell you."

She looked over at him, noticing the deepening of his tone. "What is it?"

"Sigyn and I," Loki said, his eyes raised to the sky above, the sun resting deeply against his dark skin, "we will be leaving the company."

Astrid almost jerked on the reins. "*What*?" she snapped. "Do not tell me this is because of what Thor said back in Svartalfheim!"

"Why shouldn't it be?"

"You told me how long you have served the Bleeding Throne," Astrid said, her voice straining as sadness was already grasping at her throat. "You *told* me that—"

"He called me a usurper." Loki's eyes found her, and the darkness within them was unlike what it should have been. "I cannot remain at court, I cannot remain alongside the Aesir. Not...not with Thor at its helm."

"He is only a prince."

Loki's hands tightened over the reins. "I will kill him, Astrid," he whispered with a trembling voice. "I will kill him just for the way he looks at you. Can't you understand? Can't you see what it is I am burdened with?"

Astrid pulled her eyes away from him, stunted by the intensity behind his words. She could hardly speak, hardly find the voice to whisper the cowardly words she managed to scrounge up. "What of the company?"

Loki's laugh was light and airy. "There is a place," he said, "upon the outskirts of Asgard. It is vast, full of fields and rolling hills. Compared to the golden city, you wouldn't call it much, but it is home. At least, it will be home." He let out a sigh. "The company died the moment Thor decided we would be his thralls, not his brothers and sisters in arms. I pray you might see that soon, my beloved farmer girl. You have..." Loki turned his face away, his last words to her muffled. "You have taken a place in my old, aged heart."

Just like that, Loki pulled at the reins and clicked his teeth together. The horse reared back before curving in the opposite direction, back the way they came. Astrid turned to see his steed gallop to catch up with Sigyn's, who was already disappearing into the distance. She supposed the sorceress was no good at goodbyes, or at least, that's what she preferred to tell herself. Astrid watched them for as long as she could, till Thor's sharp whistle called out to her.

And she pushed her steed forward, toward the prince, toward the golden city, not knowing at all what the road ahead looked like.

Follow Astrid through Midgard and Valhalla in her next journey...

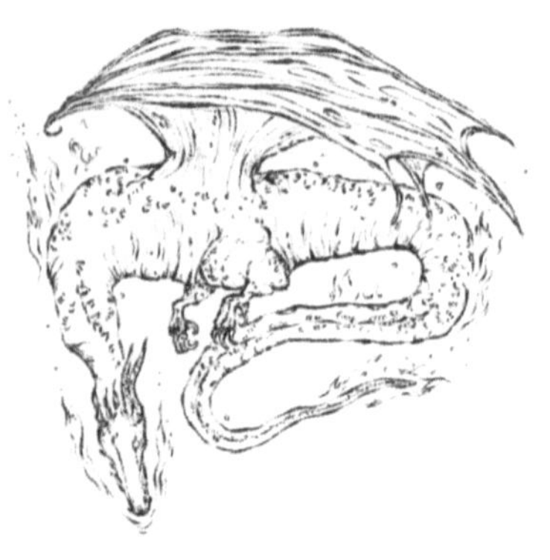

Out now!

THE DAY WE DIE

It was midnight, stifling, the bruise forming on his lip throbbing, and Milo Bohr might've been slightly high on painkillers, but that girl - that girl right over there - was her. *The* her.

She was as familiar as a recurring dream. He would know - most nights, he'd wake drenched in sweat with her face faint behind his eyelids. But there, in the shadowy room, she looked perfect: shoulders rounded down, head cocked to the right, nose an inch from her pen. Her fingers were nimble and slender; even from his distance, Milo could see the deep callouses lining her skin, grooves, and bumps along her fingertips. Chestnut hair fell from her shoulder. Absolutely one hundred percent absorbed. Milo's chest swelled with a painful euphoria. She was close, down the bar, and silent at her high top.

Reality lurched up his throat like a toad. There he sat, feigning drunkenness in the crowd to blend in, mesmerized by a nameless woman, a spun and threaded face stripped from his memory—an ethereal being plaguing his nightmares, suddenly alive, as physically apparent as he. The dreams on their own proved ridiculous: a limitless tower catching flames, ashen snow surrounding a frozen lake, and hands stained with blood. She remained the only constant: beautiful and haunting and earth-shattering. He ripped his gaze away.

The bar, known as *Carson's* to the locals and sleazy nightclub to the tourists, was home to none other than high school graduates. Loaded with fake IDs and unwarranted enthusiasm, young adults entering the real world swarmed to Carson's after the morning's cheery commencement ceremony, leaving behind the chattering and crying family members. Cheap booze and blaring EDM was the prize for twelve grueling years, only for it all to begin again at sunrise.

"Me-low!" Oba, the only person alive who could pronounce Milo's name wrong, clobbered up to the bar. The Nigerian native slapped his hand against the wood, flashing a pearly grin towards the bartender. His shout was incoherent, jumbled, and muffled against the music. The bartender, sour-faced and tired, responded with water. Oba shrugged. "What do you think?" He motioned to his clothes, the second outfit from his newly adopted 90s fashion phase: wide-legged jeans and a baggy muscle tank top. Against his Abraham Lincoln beard, piercings galore, and blemish-free skin, nothing stopped Oba from being the most enthralling person in the room. "Too much?"

"Never too much." Milo winked. "Not *enough*."

Oba jumped onto the stool beside him, clumsily knocking his elbow into a beer glass. The bartender, once again too relaxed to care, ignored the spill. "Where's your drink?"

"Designated driver."

His friend grinned, reached over the counter, and waved his hand frantically in the air to grab the bartender's attention. "Whiskey." Oba's voice was faint. "Calm the nerves."

He nodded. The anxiety medication he took this morning wore off hours ago, between graduates tossing their caps to the sky and his mother crying as her camera flashed. He eyed the glass, liquid glistening a bronze cream. "How'd you know?"

"You've got the look," said Oba.

Milo smiled. "The look."

"Like the world's fallin' on your shoulders." He motioned for Milo to drink.

He swallowed a mouthful, the heat spreading to his stomach. "What if it was?"

"Don't go existential on me, Bohr."

He sunk to the counter, its wood soothingly cool against his cheek. He saw the nameless girl's distorted figure through the whiskey glass, rippling like she was made of the ocean. A heaviness settled upon his side as he lay there, staring at her and intensely aware of Oba's steady gaze. His lips parted, breath fogging up the glass, and she disappeared. "I think I'm going crazy," he whispered.

"You had one sip, man."

"I'm not drunk."

Oba's lips pressed together. "Are you sure?"

"Do me a favor," his hand snapped over, latching onto Oba's wrist, "is she really there?"

"Who?"

"*Her.*"

Oba swiveled around. "The brunette?"

He nodded.

"She's there, buddy." He swung back. "And totally out of your league, by the way."

Milo lifted his head above the glass. "Is it possible to know someone before knowing them?"

"You mean, like, fate?"

"Is it possible?"

Oba looked away. "Does it matter?"

He fixed his gaze on her. Alarm bells reverberated against his temples, a headache boisterously growing within his skull. No matter how much it hurt, he could not turn away or make any decision that was not already written out before him. Her eyes scored his dreams, now real and there, waiting. He wasn't quite sure what he said to Oba, but it left his friend patting him on the shoulder, an encouraging look in his dark eyes.

Standing from the seat, Milo staggered across the room, the whiskey glass loose between his fingertips. He glanced at his reflection: black curls pulled behind his ears, sharp angles protruding from his face, giving off a hauntingly gaunt look. Stormy gray eyes stared back at him, squared glasses smudged and dirty, and the massive bruise formed on his bottom lip discolored a deep purple over tanned skin. *Good enough*, he thought. *And if not, it'll have to do.*

She was oblivious to his arrival, still staring at her paper, dragging the pen silently.

The glass rattled when he set it down. Her head jolted. He sunk into the seat, moving slowly and clumsily. She stared. People bumped into his back as they squeezed into the bar, laughing while he lurched forward. Heat, like the alcohol's burn, erupted in his throat, spreading across his collar and assaulting his neck. He sipped whiskey, hoping to find relief. The girl sat her pen down. Milo's heart banged against his chest. A shaking hand reached to his collar, pulling it aside as sweat trickled down his back.

"Damn you, pills," he muttered, touching the painkillers sitting so guilty in his pocket.

She turned. "Sorry?"

He cleared his throat. "Nothing from me." He glanced at her, quickly investigating how her lips curved as her eyebrows bunched together. He peeled his gaze away.

"Okay, then." Her Scottish accent rolled off the tongue like syrup.

He watched as she moved back to the paper. She scored the page with unusual marks. Considering starting a conversation, Milo contemplated his next words, suddenly realizing the lack of things he had to say. Either way, he kept getting the increasingly alarming notion that he would have something to regret if he spoke.

The pen slammed against the table. "I'm sorry, but do I know you?"

He shook his head. "If you knew me, we probably wouldn't be talking right now."

"Who said we were talking?"

He smirked. "Is this not talking, or do you have a different definition than I do?"

"Are you one of those creep guys waiting to slip something in my drink?"

His eyebrows lifted. The only glass on the table was his own. "No," he said, "thought you could use the company."

"I'm plenty involved in my work."

Milo looked at the paper. "Scribbles?" His fingers traced the same lines on the table.

"If that's what you want to call it." Her eyes gravitate towards his fingers, watching with a firm frown.

He chewed on his mouth, twirling the glass around absent-mindedly. Condensation trickled down his fingers. He tapped the table, wondering how long it would take him to burst, rambling with crazy questions about dreams and her existence. As the glass teetered around, threatening to spill across the wood, her eyes following his movements, he realized he didn't want to know it. He didn't want the truth or reality, the tainted danger lying behind her eyes, the mystery in her appearance, and her role within his life. He steadied the glass, eyes snapping to meet her own. He wanted the lie. "Do you believe in fate?"

Her frown deepened. "That's what you're going with? Got my attention in a smelly bar filled with rowdy kids, and you go with that?"

"Still got your attention," he said, "don't I?"

Her mouth gaped open, but she quickly shut it. Her expression softened. "Something's there," she said, "*out* there. Watching our moves and planning what happens next. Whether we follow it or not is on us."

Milo watched her.

"And you?"

He sighed, settling into the creaking wooden chair. "I think there's this selfish thing trying to be a god. But instead, it fucks up every single thing on this planet."

"Right," she drawled, "you're a nihilist."

"I prefer the term 'hopeful nihilist'." He leaned forward. "Nothing has meaning, right? We go day by day; thousands die, and thousands are born. Nature moves through time in this cycle, a pattern of order. No matter what, the pattern continues. We, pieces of this natural order, believe we have this sense of free will, despite seeing the loop everything else is played on, despite knowing nothing we do changes that."

"I hope this gets hopeful at some point."

He grinned. "The key to surviving the inevitable is passion."

"Passion."

"What's the biggest f– you that you can give to a primordial being called fate? Having a passionate life with passionate people." He fell back against his seat. "My high school graduation was this morning, and I tripped over the gown to fall on my face in front of the whole student body." He reached up, poking at the bruise on his bottom lip. "I'm taking all these meds cause my Mom freaked out, but my mouth is still sore." He shrugged. "This shit would've happened whether my shoes were tied or not. It's how fate works. But you know what? It didn't bother me 'cause I am sitting here, feeling like my soul is on fire."

When he looked at her, her smile lit up the room. Air poured into his lungs, a strong awareness of being there in that moment seeping into him. The sudden surge of being alive, realizing one exists within reality, shocked him, rattling him as though he was only made of bones. She smiled at him, and his vision became sharp, the heavy weight of exhaustion raised from his shoulders. He returned it as much as he could. "What?"

"Nothing," she said. "Just interesting. Unusual."

"I'll take that as a compliment."

"Good. That's what I meant."

He wanted to scream with glee.

"Did you plan on introducing yourself sometime tonight?"

"That was my next line," he said. "Milo Bohr."

She frowned. Seeing the sudden unhappiness triggered something dark within him. He pinched himself so hard blood stained his nails. *How could I have made her stop smiling?* He nervously popped the bones in his hand, opening his mouth to let the sarcasm tumble between them. "Sorry, does my name not fit your standards?"

"Look," she began while packing her things, "you're tipsy, high, and infuriating, so go home."

"Infuriating?"

Her hand twitched. "Go home, Milo."

The mystery girl from his dreams was gone. His head fell onto the bar counter with a loud *thud*. Pain throbbed through his forehead. "*Ouch.*"

"That was harsh."

Milo struggled to lift his head. Oba took over the girl's seat, lingering booze faint on his breath. "Thought I was doing good."

"You were," he said. "I *think* you were."

He covered his face. There was an annoying smudge on his glasses, but his hands weighed a million pounds, and he had no urge to clean them. Let them be dirty. He aimed for full dramatics. It was one of those nights.

"I should take you home, then." Oba jumped down from the stool.

"You're drunk!"

"No more than you, my friend. Come on."

With Oba's arm holding him up, Milo let his friend guide him out of the crowded bar as their classmates screamed and shouted excitedly. The normal Manhattan rush common during the day had no place that night. His senses were on high alert. He wanted the silence to become noise and noise to be silent. *It's just the pills*, he thought, *just the pills.*

A sharp ring came from his pocket. Oba retrieved his phone for him, glancing at the screen to see who called. He furrowed his brow and passed the phone to Milo. "It's your mother," Oba said.

Milo raised it to his ear, suddenly terrified of sounding drunk. He doubted his mother, Natalie Bohr, would mind much if he had a few drinks with friends after the commencement ceremony.

But something in him reeked of shame, and an unbearable fear of making her frown overtook him. He regretted going out rather than staying home with her. That was the shame. It had only been the two of them, but he chose to venture out of his comfort zone and go to the bar. She never showed disappointment if she felt it. He bred his shame.

"Mom," he blurted.

"Honey?" Her sweet voice became muddled in the weather. The wind rushed around them, and droplets landed on his forehead. "It's storming here. Are you inside?"

"Yeah, Mom," he lied.

"Are you feeling okay?" Her voice sounded suspicious. "You sound off."

Milo dragged his hand across his mouth as though it would erase the whiskey he had. "I'm good, Mom, really. It-it's just been a long day."

She sighed lightly. "I know, honey. I thought you could get back soon, and we could talk."

"Sure, sure," he muttered, distracted at Oba, who was slowly walking into the empty street.

"Are you listening to me?"

"Mhm."

"Milo," she said sternly this time. "It's an important talk."

"I understand, Mom," he tried to peel his eyes away from Oba, but something about how he lurked through the shadows put him on edge. "I'll be there, okay? We'll talk."

She was silent for a moment. "Okay, Milo."

"I won't let you down, Mom."

"Okay," she whispered.

"I'll see you soon."

"I love you, Milo."

He smiled. "I love you more."

The phone clicked, and the call ended. A pit of dread grew in his stomach at the call for a reason he couldn't identify. He fumbled, searching the nighttime for his friend.

"It's raining." Oba sounded miles away.

Everything was numb and unreal, nothing and everything touching him all at once. His glasses clouded with steam. Swiping them quickly along his shirt, he replaced them to see wet smudges. He felt his clothes. *Drenched.* Looking at the sky, he saw the streetlights blur with pelting rain. He staggered. Oba's guiding presence disappeared. Like a hollow bullet casing, previously filled with destruction, he echoed with air.

Milo breathed deep, the rain and the city wafting over him like a wave. Calmness washed through him, and he looked towards the unrelenting rain. He extended his hand in the motion's blur, reaching for the foggy face that formed before him—the girl from the bar. The rain became sharper, and he looked away. Manhattan towers grew sharp in his eyesight, stark silhouettes like blocks in the moonlight. Darkness shaded over him.

The world became stagnant.

Milo shuddered. A stillness wrapped around him as though the world knew what was coming without telling him.

A hand grazed against his elbow. Milo lifted his rain-soaked face to Oba. His beard flattened against his chin, and his lips moved, but Milo couldn't make it out. He opened his mouth, only a sigh left.

"Do you understand?" Oba's voice strained.

Milo squinted at him. "*What?*"

Oba looked angry. He turned his head to stare at something across the empty street. Milo felt his eyes widen - something was wrong with Oba's head. Veins extruded from beneath his skin. Thickly with wood and stone, antlers had erupted from his buzzed hair, extending into the sky above him like arms. The veins were moving, growing, spreading across the thin skin along Oba's cheeks. Rain slid down his midnight body like paint, colors bouncing around his figure like a halo. Milo fought the urge to laugh.

Fear was far from his mind. He stepped back to see the man before him in full, and his jaw dropped. Wondrous colors exploded around them and into the air. The rain roared momentarily, pulling and pushing Milo around as though fists pelted into him. Oba's figure changed and warped as he moved, trying to steady himself in the rain's onslaught.

Three things, then, became frighteningly clear.

First, Milo's best friend - scratch that, his *only* friend - was a giant with deep oceanic skin, stark antlers, and swirling eyes that held galaxies.

Second, he found himself outrageously and incoherently falling for the girl from the bar.

And lastly, with a sudden awareness that chilled him to the bone, he was going to die.

"What's happening, Oba?"

The rain lightened, and Milo's senses came back, sharpening reality. Oba reached above nine feet, clothes shredded and piercings flung away. His giant form blocked out the moon like an eclipse. Everything settled in Milo's chest. Rationality took control: fear became his number one emotion, and nothing stopped him from doing what he did next.

Oba's words came to him like booms of thunder. "It's time to _"

Milo ran.

Milo pelted by, the fallen rainwater splashing at his feet, cutting Oba's voice off. The ground shook and cracked as the giant pursued, sending tremors quaking through Milo's body. And, as though wings had sprouted from his shoulder blades, he wondered what flying would be like.

Milo, however, had an asthmatic history and was currently still getting over the fact he took too many painkillers earlier and didn't get very far. The ground shook, and Milo's legs faltered, sending him crashing down. Rolling onto his back, Milo squinted at the stars. Orion's constellation became clear, forming like a clay figure in his mind. His mother told him, once, during the early hours of the night, that his father could spend hours watching the stars; he held his hands over his eyes like binoculars. The stars looked closer for a second. He smiled. To be a star. Milo blinked - it was happening.

Oba's statuesque, giant form suddenly blocked out the stars. Everything about him looked the same, excluding the protruding veins and blue-tinted skin. Oba brought his face down towards Milo's, hot breath fanning him. "The Warriors of Thunder," he snarled, teeth ragged and sharp, *"where are they?"*

Milo considered crying. He read once that crying humanizes a person to danger's face. A shooter would be less likely to kill a girl who screams her name. Or how many fish she had. How bad her grades were. He frowned. *Why do I remember that?* It didn't matter - no tears were in stock to shed. There he was with an aching pain in his back, a wheeze escaping his lips now and then, his best friend - who *might've* been lying about who he was - standing over him, and all he could think about was two things. His mother sat in her rocking chair positioned by the front door, reading - but not *actually* reading - her latest Entertainment Weekly magazine, waiting nervously for her son to unlock the door.

And her, obviously - it always *had* to be her. He was thinking about her. Milo blinked and imagined her almond-shaped eyes staring back at him, glistening against the bar's dying lights as cheesy pop music played in the background. A girl he barely knew but had haunted his dreams for weeks was on his mind while death stood before him. He imagined it to be wonderful to reach out and touch his fingertips across her cheek's curve. Those chestnut curls would drop through his hands like honey. Milo was seconds from reaching out with his hand towards that foggy figment of his imagination.

"The Warriors of Thunder," Oba repeated. "Where are they?"

Milo thought about crying again but only felt empty as Oba raised his oversized fist. Was there a moment when life crossed that line between fiction and reality? He searched for it like a beggar, hands outstretched and wanting. And then he realized he stood with a foot on either side, waiting for something to rock him toward that inevitable ending. His heart pounded weakly against his rib cage as a monster held his thin, mundane life in his hands like a string.

He wondered what it would feel like. When he was little, he imagined thunderous wolves whisking away his father, which was why he was never around. On other days, he saw himself, older with white strands running through the curls, walking with wolves at his hips and a menacing raven hovering above his head. It didn't matter, though. There were no wolves or ravens. Instead, Oba's boulder-sized fist was hanging above like the moon, soaring down with an unstoppable force, down upon Milo Bohr.

Darkness overtook him, and death silenced his thoughts with a charismatic smile.

There was a whisper. A spring breeze washed across a field with blooming flowers, sending seeds soaring. It was soft, quiet, almost unintelligible, but at the same time, as clear as day. A singular note carried on the clouds. It crossed the dark chasm surrounding him, bounced, and echoed until it landed. He reached, but nothing moved. It echoed.

Milo.

He swore he heard a shout. It wasn't a cry, but loud and filled with rage. A horse's gallop followed it, clobbering footsteps ripping across a stone street. Another yell, a screeching war cry, erupts through his ears. The power it held echoed and burnt like a billowing fire.

Come back.

There was a lulling pull. In the darkness, Milo felt as though a rope was tied around his waist, and someone on the other end yanked, sending him jerking backward constantly. All that lay between him and beyond was the urge to remain within the darkness, sleep, and heal till he never wanted to get up again. He ignored the lull for a moment. He forgot about it. He wished to cut the rope.

And then he heard her.

Wake up.

Milo Bohr opened his eyes.

ACKNOWLEDGEMENTS

There is something devilish about this book. If you were to give me a copy of this book a year ago, and ask me if I believed it to have been written by me, I would have blatantly and unwaveringly said *no*. But perhaps there was a temptation, somewhere, within my life that I had yet to truly notice. I believe it was always in there, waiting for the right moment to spring out and onto the surface. I have learned a lot over the past year, after publishing *The Halls of Valhalla*. The indie author and reader community opened their arms to me, and I grew to discover the things I *could* do, the things I *want* to do.

So, thank *you*. Thank you for reading this book, for giving Astrid and her company of Nordic gods and goddesses a chance. Her story is incredibly special to me, and it continues on in so many ways. You made every word possible.

Thank you to everyone who read *The Warrior and Her Divine* before its release, delivering fantastic reviews and the most spectacular advice. The confidence your honest opinions give me is out of this world!

And, most of all, thank you to Kyle. Love would mean nothing without you.

About the Author

Gabriella Dennany has been a writer since grade school and self-published at 14. Almost a decade later, she has returned to writing and is publishing a four-book adult urban fantasy series surrounding Norse Mythology. *The Halls of Valhalla* was released in May 2024 and earned the 'Gold Book Award' from Literary Titan Review, where her writing is described as *"engaging, and her imaginative take on ancient myths offers a fresh perspective that keeps readers hooked."* Living in the valleys of Virginia, Gabriella spends her free time gawking at the birds who visit her feeder and adoring her cat.